The unmistakable sound of a gunshot reverberated through the humid air.

Kadir spun away from his limousine, instinctively pulling Cassandra to him. He protected her as best he could with his body and threw them both toward the opened car door and safety. Behind them onlookers and paparazzi shouted. Cassandra screamed as they vaulted through the air and into the back seat of the limo, where he landed on top of her. His bodyguard slammed the door shut, but no more gunshots sounded.

Cassandra's cheeks reddened, and her lush lips parted slightly. One of her slender legs was caught between his, in an awkward yet somehow apt position, and she'd wrapped her arms around him. Her heart beat so hard and fast, he could feel it pounding against his own.

Two attempts on his life in two days, and all he could think about was the softness of the woman beneath him.

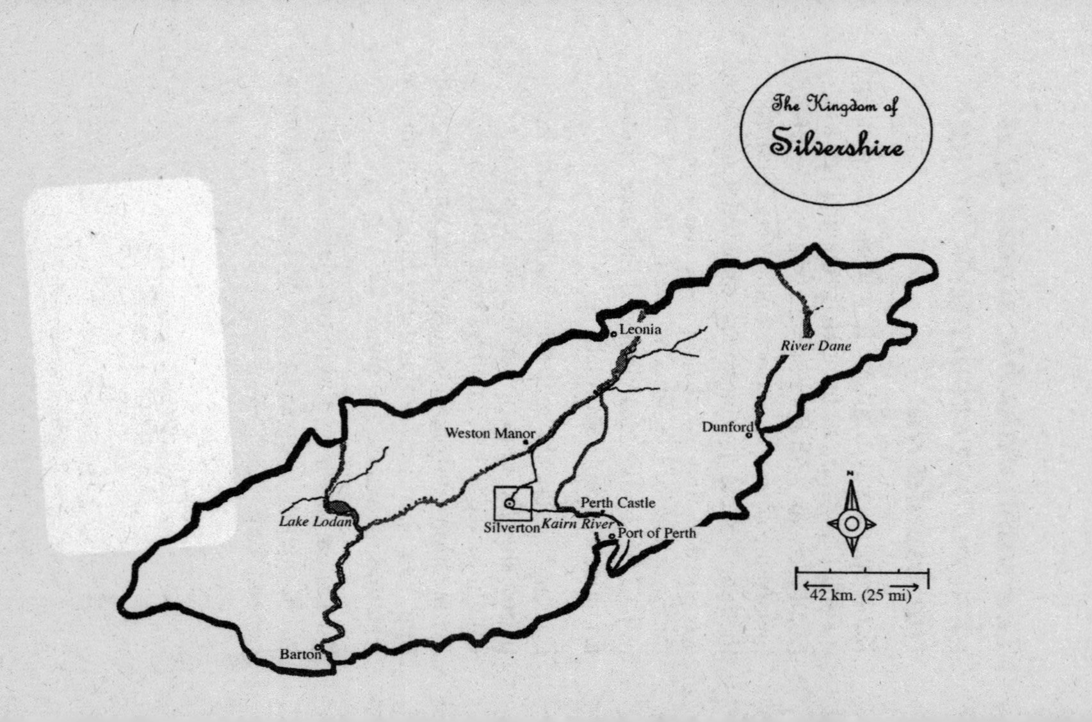

The Kingdom of
Silvershire
Leonia
River Dane
Weston Manor
Dunford
Perth Castle
Lake Lodan
Silverton
Kairn River
Port of Perth
Barton
N
42 km. (25 mi)

LINDA WINSTEAD JONES

THE SHEIK AND I

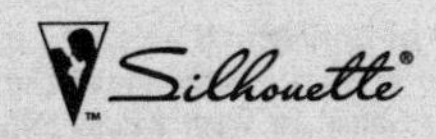

INTIMATE MOMENTS™

Published by Silhouette Books

America's Publisher of Contemporary Romance

Special thanks and acknowledgment are given to Linda Winstead Jones for her contribution to the CAPTURING THE CROWN miniseries.

ISBN 0-373-27490-4

THE SHEIK AND I

This edition published by arrangement with Harlequin Books S.A.

Visit Silhouette Books at www.eHarlequin.com

Printed in U.S.A.

Books by Linda Winstead Jones

Silhouette Intimate Moments

Bridger's Last Stand #924
Every Little Thing #1007
**Madigan's Wife* #1068
**Hot on His Trail* #1097
**Capturing Cleo* #1137
Secret-Agent Sheik #1142
**In Bed with Boone* #1156
**Wilder Days* #1203
**Clint's Wild Ride* #1217
**On Dean's Watch* #1234
A Touch of the Beast #1317
†*Running Scared* #1334
†*Truly, Madly, Dangerously* #1348
†*One Major Distraction* #1372
The Sheik and I #1420

Silhouette Books

Love Is Murder
"Calling after Midnight"

Family Secrets
Fever

*The Sinclair Connection
†Last Chance Heroes

LINDA WINSTEAD JONES

has written more than fifty romance books in several subgenres. Historical, fairy tale, paranormal and, of course, romantic suspense. She's won the Colorado Romance Writers Award of Excellence twice, is a three-time RITA® Award finalist, and (writing as Linda Fallon) winner of the 2004 RITA® Award for paranormal romance.

Linda lives in North Alabama with her husband of thirty-four years. She can be reached via www.eHarlequin.com or her own Web site, www.lindawinsteadjones.com.

For The Children.
May all your dreams come true.

Chapter 1

Kadir stood on the balcony of his villa on the sea, and watched the waves come in as the morning sun glinted on the gentle surf. From this vantage point he could usually see his yacht anchored in the near distance, but it had been gone for several days now. His crew was sailing the ship to the coast of Silvershire. Having his own familiar space available during his weeks there would make the long stay more tolerable, he was certain.

A private jet waited at a nearby airstrip, ready to carry Kadir and his retinue of bodyguards and aides to Silvershire. There he would not only attend the Founder's Day Gala to which he'd been invited; he would also meet with Lord Carrington, the apparent king-in-waiting. The old king was very ill, and his only son, Prince Reginald, had died under mysterious circumstances some months back. There were, of course, many suppositions about who had killed the obnoxious prince, and why, but Kadir paid little attention to rumor.

In truth, Kadir didn't care who ruled Silvershire. He desired an alliance with the ruler of that country—whomever he might be—in order to strengthen Kahani. Every affiliation he formed or strengthened, every handshake, every smile, every friendship brought Kahani another step into the modern world. Kadir wanted, more than anything, to see the country he loved move into the twenty-first century with dignity and strength.

There were those who wanted Kahani to turn back the clock a thousand years. Most citizens wanted nothing more than peace and prosperity. A home. Food for their loved ones. Safety for their family. But for some, that was not enough. For some, life was one battle after another, and they did not want that peace. A tightness grew in Kadir's chest. Dissidence in Kahani was not new. Zahid Bin-Asfour had been a thorn in his side for a very long time. Fifteen years and four months.

Every alliance cemented Kahani's place in the new world, but there was another reason Kadir desired a meeting with Lord Carrington. Reliable intelligence indicated that Zahid and Prince Reginald had met not long before the prince's death. Three days before, to be exact. Kadir didn't know why Zahid and the late prince had met. If Carrington had intelligence himself he did not…a sharing of information might be most useful to both parties, and both countries.

Kadir watched a familiar figure approach from the east, the sun at the old man's back. Mukhtar ran a local market and delivered fresh fruits and vegetables several times a week. He carried a canvas bag that bulged with lemons, grapes and almonds—Kadir's favorites—and whatever vegetables had looked best that morning. The bodyguards who surrounded the villa at all times were accustomed to the friendly vendor. As Mukhtar drew closer, Kadir could see that he did not wear his usual smile. He was not only in an uncustomary bad mood, but had apparently forgotten that Kadir was leaving the country today and would not return for several weeks, therefore having no need for this morning's delivery. Something must've distracted the usually pleasant man.

"Good morning," Kadir called as the man approached the balcony. Mukhtar's feet dug holes into the sand, and he kept his head bowed.

Before he reached the balcony, Mukhtar stopped. He did not raise his head.

"Is everything all right?" Kadir rushed down the steps to join the old man on the sand. "You're looking rather pale. If you need a doctor…"

Mukhtar lifted his head. There were tears in his eyes. "I'm very sorry," he croaked. "I didn't have any choice, you must understand. They have my children. My daughters, and my son. My new grandson." He shivered visibly. "I must do as they say. Forgive me."

The canvas bag Mukhtar carried bulged in such a way that Kadir knew—too late—that it did not contain the usual fruits and vegetables. Mukhtar's distressed face and the cleverly disguised handcuffs that Kadir had not seen until it was too late told him what was in that bag.

Kadir wondered, as he took a step closer to the old man, if the explosive apparatus would be triggered by a timer, a remote device or the frightened vendor himself. "Let me help you. The king's guard can rescue your family. Whoever has done this, you can be sure that he has no honor. A man who would kidnap innocents to force you to this will not release his captives, no matter what you do."

Mukhtar took a step back. "He told me you would say that. He also said I should remind you that you could not save *her*."

Kadir took a deep breath. *Zahid.* In the past few years, Bin-Asfour had spent most of his time in neighboring countries. Was he back in Kahani? Was he watching? What had precipitated this newest and boldest attempt on Kadir's life? Whatever the reason, now was not the time to allow his old enemy to taunt him into making a foolish decision. "That is the past. All that matters is now. All that matters is saving your family. I can have an explosives expert here in moments. We'll disarm the bomb, free you and set about rescuing your family. You can help me end the tyranny of a madman who wants to drag us all into the past. You can be a hero."

Mukhtar lifted his chin, and Kadir could see that his decision had been made. "Don't come any closer." He took a small step back, and then another. "I did not know what to do, Excellency. Forgive me. I am a foolish old man."

"No, you're…"

Kadir got no further before the man turned and ran. Not toward him, as was surely Zahid's intention, but away—toward the sea. The guards saw what was happening and moved forward, guns drawn, to place themselves between Kadir and the source of danger.

"Don't shoot!" Kadir called. There was no need. At the moment, Mukhtar was a threat only to himself. When he reached the edge of the water Mukhtar turned, and in that instant his eyes met Kadir's. The old man no longer cried. Instead he was stalwart and determined.

One hand moved toward the bag that was handcuffed to the vendor.

"No," Kadir whispered.

A powerful explosion rocked the peaceful morning, and those guards who were closest to the bomber were thrown backward and to the ground. None were close enough to be injured—though Sayyid appeared to be stunned by the jolting fall. The sound of the blast rang in Kadir's ears, and a cloud of sand danced where the old man had once stood. Sayyid and the others who had run to stop Mukhtar from his foolishness shook off their surprise and slowly regained their footing in the sand.

Kadir turned his back to the violence and climbed the steps to the balcony. Household servants and political aides who had been preparing for the upcoming trip ran onto the balcony and were met with horror.

Kadir did not look back at the beach, as he had no desire to see what was left of a decent man. He caught his personal secretary's eyes and issued a command. "Get Sharif Al-Asad on the telephone." Sharif was a highly placed officer with the Ministry of Defense. He and Kadir had once worked together, but years ago their careers had taken very diverse paths. Still, they had managed to remain friends. Their methods of operation were different, but their ultimate goals were much the same.

Hakim nodded curtly, snapping, "Yes, Excellency," before returning to the house to do as he was told.

The others remained on the balcony, watching the scene on the beach in horror and surprise. There should be no surprise at unexpected violence, but horror...yes. An old man blowing himself up in a vain attempt to save his family was the height of horror.

Kadir had sacrificed much in the name of what was best for Kahani. He was thirty-six years old and had no wife, no children. There had been a steady succession of women in his life, all of them fun for a while but in the end…uninspiring. He could easily arrange a marriage with a suitable woman he had never met, but that would mean calling upon the ways of the past. Ways he was determined to change.

His parents were gone, and his brothers had lives and families of their own. And of late, Kadir was not always certain of what he most wanted. One thing was certain: He wanted Zahid Bin-Asfour destroyed. He would not rest easy until that was done.

Hakim had Sharif on the line within minutes, and Kadir shared all the information he could, as he set the rescue of Mukhtar's family into motion. There had been a time when he would have been one of the men storming the terrorist camp in order to rescue the innocent, but these days his role in defeating terrorism took a different slant.

When Kahani was properly and securely aligned with a number of powerful nations who would come to their aid when the need arose, Zahid and those who followed him would be reduced to nothingness. These days, Kadir did his best to defeat his enemies in a different way—with a smile, a handshake and the sincere promise of alliance.

Zahid Bin-Asfour could not fight the entire world, and Kadir intended to bring that world down on his head.

"He's a *what?*" Lexie plopped down onto the couch.

Cassandra glanced at her sister. Of all the possible mornings for an unannounced visit, this had to be the worst. "You heard me the first time."

"A sheik," Lexie said with a grin. "A genuine, sweep-me-away-on-your-white-horse sheik. Very cool, Cass. What's the catch? Is he old? Married? Ugly?"

Lexie was a sweet woman, but diplomacy was nothing more than a vague concept to the eldest of the four Klein sisters. Fortunately, Silvershire foreign relations were safe from Alexis Margaret Klein Harvey Smythe Phillips, whose only agenda at the present time was finding husband number four.

Cassandra Rose Klein's ambitions had taken a different vein. She wanted to make a difference in the world. She wouldn't call herself power-hungry, but she was ambitious. It wasn't that she didn't want to love somebody, but there was more to the future than a man…or as in her sister's case, a series of men.

"He's single," Cassandra said. She grabbed the file she'd been studying over her morning coffee and tossed it onto the couch. "And *not* old."

Lexie snatched up the folder and opened it. A recent photo of Cassandra's latest assignment filled most of the first page. "Ooohhh. Not ugly at *all.*" She read aloud, "'His Excellency Sheik Kadir Bin Arif Yusef Al-Nuri, Director of European and American Affairs for the Kahani Ministry of Foreign Affairs.'" Her nose wrinkled. "Do you have to memorize all that?"

"Yes."

"What will you call him? Kadir? Yusef? Arif? Honeybunch? What?"

"I'll address him as Excellency, unless he invites me to call him Sheik Kadir."

Lexie leafed through the rest of the file, not at all interested in what was truly important. She didn't care what Al-Nuri had done for his country, or what he wanted to do in the future. Lexie didn't care about politics, reform, or alliances. She only noticed Al-Nuri's physical attributes. If she had even a clue what his bank account looked like…

"How did you get so lucky?" Lexie asked as she closed the file. "I understand when it comes to politics, blackmail works wonders. Or are you sleeping with your boss?"

Cassandra laughed. "My boss is a very small, very sour woman who's probably old enough to be my grandmother."

"Weren't all the diplomatic aides fighting over who'd get him? Taking charge of the sheik for the next couple of weeks is not exactly going to be a chore."

Cassandra took a deep, calming breath. "I was given this assignment because I'm fluent in Arabic and I'm familiar with Kahani customs. Don't let your imagination run amok. My relationship with Al-Nuri will be strictly business."

"Everything is strictly business with you, Cass," Lexie teased. "Doesn't that get boring after a while?"

"I didn't enter foreign service so I could meet men."

"You can't tell me you don't find the sheik the least bit attractive."

Cassandra remained cool. "It doesn't matter if he's attractive or not."

"Of course it matters," Lexie said with an aggravated sigh. "You're twenty-five years old, and I can't remember the last time you were the slightest bit serious about the opposite sex. What are you waiting for?"

Love. Cassandra bit her lip and didn't answer aloud. Lexie had been involved in one destructive relationship after another since the day she'd turned seventeen. She knew no caution where love was concerned.

Cassandra, the youngest of the Klein sisters, knew nothing *but* caution. She also knew hope, though it rarely showed. How many times had her mother told her about the first time she'd seen the man she'd immediately known she was destined to spend a lifetime with? A glance across a crowded café. A fluttering of the heart and an inexplicable feeling of familiarity followed, then came an out-and-out flip of the stomach. Two months after that meeting they were married. A year later, Lexie had been born. Growing up, that story of love at first sight had been the fairy tale for Cassandra.

She'd been waiting from the age of fourteen for the fluttering and flipping of her insides, but she had begun to think it would never come. There had been no glance across a crowded room. No butterflies in the stomach. No swelling of love at the sight of a face, no breath held in anticipation at the sound of a voice.

Lexie rose and reached into her handbag. She came up with a jangling key chain. "Here." She tossed the keys and Cassandra caught them. "In case you want to take the hunky sheik to my beach house. I won't be back for a month."

"Where are you going?"

"I'm going to Greece, with Stanley."

Cassandra bit her lip. She didn't like Stanley Porter, Lexie's latest love interest, but Lexie wouldn't listen to her little sister's concerns. "Be careful."

"You're the one who needs to be careful. That sheik of yours is a ladies' man."

"How can you tell from one photograph—"

"The eyes," Lexie interrupted. "Your sheik has bedroom eyes, Cass. One proper glance from eyes like those, and a woman doesn't stand a chance."

For this afternoon's initial meeting Cassandra had chosen her most austere gray suit, and her long pale hair was pulled back in a neat French braid. Her heels were low and comfortable. This was a big assignment, the most important of her career, and she was ready to take it on. "His Excellency does have a bit of a reputation as a playboy. Nothing I can't handle." She dangled the keys to the beach house Lexie had gotten in her second divorce. "I won't need these."

Lexie didn't take the keys as she passed on her way to the front door of Cassandra's small but neat flat, chosen because it was affordable and less than ten minutes from the building where the Silvershire Ministry of Foreign Affairs was located. "Keep them anyway, just in case. Maybe you'll get lucky. I keep condoms in the master bathroom cabinet, under the sink."

For a moment, Cassandra considered tossing the keys at her sister's back, but that wasn't her style.

When she collected the file on Al-Nuri from the coffee table, she glanced at the photograph that had so impressed Lexie. His Excellency had a nicely trimmed mustache and beard on a ruggedly handsome face. Wavy dark hair barely touched broad shoulders, and his olive complexion was warm. But it was the eyes that drew and held her attention. Bedroom eyes, Lexie called them. *Is this literally what a man's eyes look like in the bedroom?* A shiver walked down Cassandra's spine, and the hairs on the back of her neck stood and danced.

She had no idea what a man looked like in that situation, and at the current rate of her nonexistent love life, she'd never find out.

* * *

Cassandra paced in the shade of a hangar. Al-Nuri's plane was scheduled to land at this small, private airport in less than fifteen minutes.

This new wrinkle was alarming, but she felt up to the task. If she wanted to rise in the ranks, she could not allow any twist or turn to alarm or distress her. If she became the aide who was able to handle any situation—even this one—she would soon be indispensable.

More than anything, Cassandra wanted to be indispensable.

His Excellency, Sheik Kadir, had requested a meeting with Lord Carrington, to take place as soon as possible. For a variety of reasons, Lord Carrington was not yet ready to meet with the sheik. Just as she had been about to leave for the airport, Cassandra had been asked by her superior, Ms. Nola Dunn, to keep the man entertained—no, *distracted* was a better word—until such a time came that the meeting was desirable for both parties.

Cassandra didn't know precisely why Lord Carrington didn't want to meet with his visitor from Kahani just yet, but she did know that something important was going on in the palace. Something to which a woman of her station would not be privy. There was an electricity among those in the know, an unnatural energy that kept them all on edge. Even Ms. Dunn had been edgy.

It didn't matter. One day she would be privy to everything. One day.

Cassandra knew this assignment could make or break her career in foreign service. For years, she'd studied other cultures and languages in hopes that one day she would be Silvershire's representative around the world, in places where the small country she called home had never held a position of importance. For now she was a low-level diplomatic aide, but one day—one day she would see the world.

She had done her best to make herself valuable in her present station, hoping to be noticed and promoted. During the latest computer upgrade, she'd stayed late almost every day, making sure everyone's station was in proper working order, if they asked her to help. They often did, since she was quite good with computers, and always available to assist. When Ms. Dunn's latest disaster of a secretary had made a mess of her files, Cassandra had volunteered to work on the weekends until order was restored. She was very good at restoring order.

Keeping up with news from around the world was quite important, and was a big part of her job. She had bulging files on all the countries that would be represented at the upcoming Founder's Day Gala, and she'd shared what she'd gathered with the others in the office. Still, none of the assignments she'd taken on to this point were as important as this one.

She recognized the sheik's jet as it landed and taxied toward the hangar. The flag of Kahani was proudly painted on the side of the jet. The time of the sheik's arrival had been a carefully guarded secret, so there was no fanfare, and no curious onlookers clamored for a peek of the entourage. There was just her, and a driver who waited in the parking lot on the other side of the hangar. Cassandra straightened her spine and took a deep breath of air. Not only did she have to assist the foreign minister from Kahani with a fine balance of respect for his customs as well as respect for her own, now she had to stall him in his quest for a meeting with the duke. Too bad Lexie had already left the country.

She was an expert at keeping men of all types diverted. Cassandra had never been good at diversion. She was much better suited to directness...often to the point of bluntness. Why be subtle when directly spoken words were so much more, well, direct?

If Lexie was a soft feather of seduction and distraction, Cassandra was a mallet.

The jet came to an easy halt on the runway. After a short pause, the door opened and a stair was lowered. For a moment no one descended. Cassandra's nerves were none the better for the delay. She'd just as soon get this difficult assignment under way.

A tall, thin man in a severe dark suit was first down the stairs. He studied the area as he descended, one hand held ready over his right hip, where a weapon no doubt was housed in a holster of some type. At a crisp word from the tall man, two others descended the stairway—more quickly and not quite as openly aware. Cassandra stepped toward the jet, and immediately had the attention of all three men. She could see that they instantly assessed her as nonthreatening, but they were prepared for anything. No one answered her smile.

"Good afternoon," she said, speaking in perfectly accented Arabic. "I'm Cassandra Klein, and I will be His Excellency's guide during his stay in Silvershire." She received no response from the men, none of whom was the sheik she had been sent here to meet. Was it possible that he had canceled his appearance and one of these men was his replacement? No, these men were muscle. Bodyguards, no doubt. Kahani wasn't the hotbed of terrorism some of the neighboring countries had become, but neither was it an entirely safe place. Leaders who worked to bring about change were often endangered, and she imagined Al-Nuri was no exception to that rule.

She heard a soft, deep voice from just inside the jet, and a moment later a man she recognized as Sheik Kadir appeared at the top of the stairs. Another guard was positioned behind him, and she caught a glimpse of two others—not muscle, from what little she saw of them. They were administrative assistants, no doubt. From the top of the stairs, the sheik looked down at her and smiled. Cassandra's stomach did an unexpected flip. Her heart fluttered. Oh, dear, the man's photos did not do him justice, not at all. Her smile remained in place, a wooden mask as she gathered her wits about her. Her stomach only flipped because she'd eaten that salad dressing at lunch. It had tasted good enough, but obviously it had gone bad. She steeled her heart against another flutter as the man she had been sent here to meet descended the stairs with the grace of an athlete and the smile of a movie star. Like the others, he was dressed in an expensive suit that fit him perfectly. Unlike the others, he continued to smile.

"What a pleasure to be greeted by such beauty."

Cassandra hated it when someone, *anyone,* commented on her physical appearance, when whether or not she was pretty had nothing to do with diplomatic service. But of course, she could say nothing to reprimand the sheik.

Oh, my, those eyes. Bedroom eyes, Lexie had called them, and so close...yes, that description made sense. In a moment of utter insanity her innards began to react again, and an unexpected and unwanted thought flitted through her mind.

He's the one.

No, Cassandra insisted to herself as she pushed her surprising reaction aside. Aside and down with a vengeance, until it was buried deep. The dance of her stomach, the knot in her chest, it was surely nothing more than the ill effects of bad salad dressing. She couldn't allow it to be anything else.

Chapter 2

Kadir gave a curt bow to the woman who was waiting at the foot of the jet's stairway. He'd received a communication days ago giving him the woman's name, so her gender was no surprise. He had not, however, expected that she would be so beautiful. Though she dressed in a conservative suit, and her shoes were of the sensible sort, and her pale blond hair was twisted back in a severe style that only accentuated her fine cheekbones and large gray eyes, she exuded an unexpected sensuality he could not ignore. The day had not been a pleasant one thus far, so it was surprisingly enjoyable to get lost in her beauty for a moment.

"Excellency," she said, her voice professional and curt. "Welcome. It's my pleasure to be given the opportunity to assist you during your stay in Silvershire. A car is waiting." She indicated the direction of the car with a wave of her delicate hand. "Whatever you require during your stay with us, you need only to ask."

What he required as a man was very different from what he needed as a diplomat. He'd had little time or opportunity to care for the man in himself these past few years. Unfortunately, that fact had not changed.

"I understand an estate near the palace has been prepared for me and my staff."

"Yes." Ms. Klein led the way to the waiting limousine while Sayyid and Fahd collected the luggage from the jet. "The Redmond Estate. Mr. Redmond and his new wife are vacationing in Paris and will not return for several months, and they graciously offered their home. I understand your guard detail has already been informed of the existing security system."

"Yes. They believe it will be satisfactory."

Since his yacht was anchored near a small shore town a relatively short distance from the palace, he would be able to slip away on occasion. Living in someone else's home was often awkward. He preferred his own quarters, even if they were small rooms on a modest but familiar seagoing vessel.

"It's very kind of the Redmonds to offer their home. Hotels are so impersonal and..." Dangerous, though he did not tell her as much. He did not normally concern himself overmuch with safety issues, but this morning's incident made it clear that Zahid was determined to remove Kadir from the picture. "Shall we say, they do not have the warmth of a real home. I am most appreciative."

The limousine was large enough to accommodate his entire party. Four bodyguards, his personal secretary, a junior aide from the Ministry of Foreign Affairs and himself. And Ms. Klein, of course. Tension from this morning's unfortunate episode remained, clear in each of his associates. Kadir did his best not to appear tense with his escort, who would surely take it as a sign of unease with the current situation. As a precaution, his bodyguards searched the car inside and out—and underneath—and they also searched the driver. He saw no need to explain to Ms. Klein that just this morning an attempt had been made on his life.

Once they were settled in the vehicle, and it moved away from the small airport, Kadir turned to his assigned aide and smiled. It was a diplomat's smile—wide and guarded and touched with hope. "I am looking forward to meeting with the duke. We have much to discuss."

To her credit, Ms. Klein did not blush. But he read the answer in her eyes, as they all but shut down. That gray, which had been soft as a dove's wing moments ago, grew ever so slightly harder. Given her profession, she really should be more difficult to read. She was young, however, and had time to develop a more stony expression.

What a shame that would be. He liked the expressiveness of her eyes, even when she was about to disappoint him.

"Lord Carrington's schedule is quite full at the moment, I regret to say. I'm sure he's anxious to meet with you, and will do so as soon as is possible. Until then, I hope you'll be interested in seeing more of Silvershire. It is a beautiful country, and I have a number of activities planned for the coming weeks."

Kadir had no interest in seeing more of Silvershire—or anywhere else. He would have his meeting with Carrington; it was the reason for this trip. He was not annoyed by Ms. Klein's answer, however. He would play whatever game she had planned for him.

He had a feeling games with his appointed aide would be quite interesting.

The estate where Sheik Kadir would be housed was an old and dignified home that actually resembled a small castle. It sported stone walls and well-tended gardens, rooms furnished in flawless antiques, servants around every corner and even a small, unused tower. It was very much like stepping back in time three hundred years.

The owner of the estate, Prentiss Redmond, was not titled. His money was new. Well, relatively new. His father had made a fortune in steel and oil refineries. Prentiss seemed better suited to spending money than to making it, and his new wife, who was fifteen years younger than he, would likely be glad to help him spend every dime. Redmond very much wanted to be *in* with the royals, and that was the reason he'd offered his home for the use of their guests.

The sheik's bodyguards immediately took over the estate security. They had received information about the household staff and cleared them all weeks ago. None of the servants could be considered threatening. Most of them looked as if they might've actually been here three hundred years ago.

Cassandra stifled a smile as Oscar, the ancient butler, led Al-Nuri up the wide, winding staircase. The old man moved very slowly, and with great dignity. The sheik did not seem at all perturbed to be moving at a snail's pace—and that was a definite point in his favor. While you'd think patience was a requirement of all diplomats, she had met many who had none.

She did her best to once again dismiss the physical reaction she'd had to the sheik when he'd stepped off the plane. Salad dressing, nerves, a virus coming on—it could be any of those things, and she much preferred any of them, even the virus, to the possibility of a strong physical attraction to Al-Nuri. Even though she had, at times, bemoaned the lack of love in her life, when it did come it couldn't possibly be with a man who lived in a country where women might as well be trapped in the nineteenth century—no, the *first* century! She was a thoroughly modern woman, with plans for a career. An important career.

Besides, when she experienced that feeling of love her mother had so often told her about, it really should be with a fellow citizen of Silvershire. A quiet and intelligent man—she had never cared for show-offs or comedians—who would support her in her career. And he really should be blond, so their children would all be blond. Logically she knew that setting hair color as a criteria was nonsensical, but she was grasping at straws to convince herself that the man who climbed the stairs ahead of her would not do. The sheik was more than ten years older than she. That was surely much too great an age difference for true compatibility. She mentally listed all the reasons she couldn't have any sort of physical attraction to the sheik, and it almost worked.

Then at the top of the stairs he turned and smiled at her. It was a truer smile than the one he had flashed at her earlier, and she saw what was surely a hint of the real man in that smile. He was amused by Oscar—by the pace, the uniform, the dialogue as the old butler shared the history of the mansion as they endlessly climbed the stairs. She liked that, that he could be amused. Amused, and kind enough not to hurry the older man along or reprimand him for his slowness or a tale that often rambled.

Cassandra had always prided herself on being all-business. She was the mallet, after all. The sledgehammer. The ice queen, Lexie had called her more than once. It had seemed like an insult at the time, but she could use that quality to her advantage now.

If she found that her resolve was not strong enough, she could always ask to be removed from the assignment. But how would that look on her employment record? "Resigned for reasons of uncontrollable physical attraction to a totally unsuitable man" would ruin her career.

With effort, she returned Al-Nuri's smile. "Excellency, I'm sure you'd like an opportunity to settle into your new accommodations before we begin our tour of the country. Tomorrow morning we'll visit the Maitland Museum of Fine Arts an hour before it's opened to the public. The museum opened just last year, and is quite impressive. You'll have the rest of the day today to get settled in your quarters. If there's anything you need..." She was ready to make her escape—at least for now.

"I do have many questions about the current political state of Silvershire."

Of course he had questions about the prince's death, the king's medical condition, the possibility that the duke would soon take the throne. She was prepared to answer all of his questions—within reason, of course.

"After you've settled into the estate, we'll have a chance to discuss anything you find of interest."

Oscar was continuing toward the suite of rooms that would be Al-Nuri's during his stay in Silvershire. The elderly butler was unaware that he'd lost his audience. He was mumbling about something that had taken place in this very hallway, a hundred and twenty-four years ago.

Cassandra locked eyes with the sheik, and she knew very well what he found of interest. Just because she was inexperienced, that didn't mean she was blind. She steeled her spine—again. If he intended to make this assignment difficult for her, so be it. He would find she wasn't eager for his attentions, as most women he met probably were. This was business, and their relationship would remain professional.

"Tonight," the sheik said as he turned to follow a doddering Oscar. "I'm sure dinner here in the estate can be arranged. Eight o'clock."

Cassandra was tempted to decline the invitation, but this was her job. And no man, not even this one, would make her run.

Kadir received an important phone call from Sharif late in the afternoon of his arrival in Silvershire. Intelligence indicating the location of Mukhtar's family had been obtained, thanks to a neighbor who had witnessed the kidnapping and had given a detailed description of the driver and the vehicle used. With that information, Sharif had tracked the kidnappers and Mukhtar's family to a quiet neighborhood just a few miles away from the market. The planning of the rescue operation was under way. There was no indication of whether or not Zahid was in the same location—but it was certainly possible. In the past they had been close to Bin-Asfour many times, but he always escaped, leaving his followers to suffer for his ambitions and his tendency to do violence.

Kadir very much wanted Mukhtar's family to be rescued, but in truth this wouldn't be over until Zahid was caught—or killed. No matter how many successful battles were waged, no matter how many soldiers Zahid lost—he always managed to survive. His army could be decimated, and within days he would have a new army. Bin-Asfour was known for his silver tongue, for his ability to convert otherwise sane men to his insane cause.

Kadir would love to be the one to pull the trigger and see Zahid dead, but he'd left that part of his life behind when he'd decided to be a diplomat. He could not battle for his country's future in both ways—only one. Violence required less thought, and was in many ways much easier than diplomacy. A soldier did as he was told and the results, good or bad, were immediate. In his current position he had to be cautious about every word, every decision. Yes, in many ways being a soldier was easier…but he was no longer a soldier, and very little in his life was easy.

Sharif wanted to see Bin-Asfour dead as much as Kadir did, but for his own reasons. There had been a time when they'd discussed those reasons…but no more. The time for talk was long past.

He could've ordered dinner for two to be served in the elegant formal dining room of his home-for-the-moment. Ms. Klein no doubt expected that, and would come prepared to maintain her all-business attitude toward him. She was his contact here in Silvershire, his advocate—though she did not yet see herself in that way. She was his key to gaining access to Lord Carrington, and he would do whatever was necessary to woo her to his way of thinking. In order to do that, he must first charm her.

He suspected where Ms. Klein was concerned, a gun would likely be much easier than diplomatic charm.

In order to keep her off guard, he arranged dinner for four to be served at a small table in a cozy drawing room. He invited his clerk and his aide to join him and Ms. Klein for dinner, and as with all else they complied. Sayyid and Haroun would keep watch, while Fahd and Jibril slept. They would take over at midnight, and until he left Silvershire they would maintain that schedule—two men midnight to noon, the other two noon to midnight. He was growing so accustomed to the constant presence of bodyguards, he sometimes forgot they were with him. After all, they could usually blend into the background—a necessary precaution, a part of the job.

In the past few years, Zahid had not been a direct threat. He and his followers moved from country to country, searching for and occasionally finding support for their cause. They performed acts of terrorism outside of Kahani, and at the same time they built their fortune through the sale of drugs. Kadir didn't know why Zahid had tried to have him killed at the present time, but neither could he deny the new danger. No matter how much he would like to, he could not entirely forget why he had such a close guard at hand.

It was pleasant to see the expression on Ms. Klein's face when she was escorted into the sitting room precisely at eight o'clock. She was still dressed in her severe suit, and had added no makeup or jewels to make the ensemble more appropriate for evening. It was surely her way of telling him that their relationship was purely business and would remain so. She was dedicated, in that way only the very young can be. What would it take to make sure that she was dedicated to him and his mission of meeting with the king-in-waiting?

"Thank you so much for taking the time from your busy schedule to dine with us this evening." Kadir watched as her eyes took in the small table set for four and the silent presence of his aides. She then turned her eyes to him. Was she surprised to find him dressed casually and comfortably? His pants were freshly pressed, but the shirt he had chosen was unbuttoned at the collar, and he wore no tie. He had not even trimmed his mustache and goatee, so a bristly shadow roughened a portion of face. He needed a haircut, as usual, but he was not by any means disheveled. Just casual, as if the meeting were of no real importance.

"We do have much to discuss," Ms. Klein said, almost suspiciously. "I can tell you all about the schedule for this coming week, and if you have any questions about the events surrounding the Founder's Day Gala, I'll be happy to answer them."

"Lovely." He eased her chair away from the table and waited for her to sit. After a split second of indecision she did so, and he made sure she was in place before he sat across the table from her. Hakim and Tarif took the remaining chairs, while Sayyid and Haroun maintained their posts at the two doors that opened off the small sitting room.

Kadir listened attentively as Ms. Klein told him all about her plans for the week. Museums, gardens, tours of homes much like this one. Nothing of substance, and nothing he had not seen before. He did not tell her so, of course, but smiled and expressed interest in each and every event. As the simple meal progressed, she became more and more relaxed. She was never entirely relaxed—he suspected that was not in her nature—but at least she was no longer suspicious of his motives.

After dessert, Hakim excused himself, stating that he had work to do before retiring for the night. Tarif was not far behind him. Kadir asked Ms. Klein about the state of Silvershire's public education system, and she gladly began a well-practiced and seemingly attentive diatribe.

Kahani's public education system was in bad need of an overhaul, and the subject was of great interest to him. But it wasn't long before Kadir's attention's wandered. His Silvershire aide had such attractive gray eyes, and such a wonderfully lush mouth, it was impossible to concentrate on test scores and curriculum when she was looking at him. He was not a man who could be easily distracted, but that's what Cassandra Klein did. She distracted him to the extreme.

What man would not be distracted? The suit she wore did not entirely disguise the fact that she had a nicely rounded female shape. He had hoped that at some time during the evening she would remove her suit jacket, but she had not. Of course not. She was determined to be professional and proper, which was a true waste. Her eyes were lively, and her mouth was made for better things than talking business. The lips were soft and full, and made for kissing. He wanted to see her laugh, at least once.

As nice as his wandering thoughts were, he didn't have time for such nonsense. Like the woman sitting before him, he needed to concentrate on the reasons for this visit.

"You have made such wonderful plans for my time here, and I certainly don't want to miss a single event.

I do wonder if there would be an opportunity to tour Barton College while I'm here?"

The question took her by surprise. Her eyes widened slightly, and she held her breath for a moment. "Certainly," she answered. There was a short hesitation before she added, "You do realize that Barton is a women's college."

"Of course." Ms. Klein would find that she was not the only one who came to this meeting well prepared. "If my memory is correct, Barton College was founded in 1873, and has been a school of privilege until the past seventeen years, when generous scholarships funded by the government have allowed those who otherwise would not be able to afford such a fine education to attend."

Ms. Klein looked slightly suspicious at his knowledge. "I attended Barton myself. My mother teaches there."

"Wonderful! I can expect a most thorough tour, in that case."

She cocked her head slightly. "May I ask why you wish to tour Barton?"

"Education is the answer to so many of the world's problems, don't you agree?" He didn't give her an opportunity to answer, but he read the yes in her eyes. "I am interested in forming just such a facility in Kahani. How can I work to bring my country into the new millennium without offering an adequate education for one half of our population? The educational needs of women in Kahani have been neglected for so long, it seems only right that we rectify that disservice in as practical and effective a way as possible."

She shook off her surprise quickly. "I will make the arrangements. The summer session is much smaller than fall and spring, but we can tour the facilities and meet with the dean, if you'd like."

"I would like that very much. Will I have the opportunity to meet your mother?"

Again, the question took her by surprise. He liked surprising her; her reactions were so genuine, they cracked her tough facade and revealed the woman beneath. "Perhaps."

She glanced at her watch, and appeared to be surprised at the lateness of the hour. "I really should go, Excellency." She stood quickly. "Thank you so much for dinner. I will collect you at quarter of nine in the morning, so we can begin our tour of the museum before it opens to the public."

Kadir cared nothing for museums, but did not say so. "I look forward to seeing you again." He bowed gently. "May I…"

She turned to face him as she collected her handbag from the small table by the door. Sayyid was posted just outside that door, but was out of sight.

"May you?" she prompted.

"May I call you Cassandra? It's such a lovely name, and we will be spending many hours together in the weeks to come. I would, of course, like it very much if you'd call me Kadir. 'Excellency' has never suited me. I keep looking over my shoulder for the stuffy old man who answers to that dignified title." He tried a smile, even though the woman who was poised to flee didn't look as if she were about to say yes to his proposal. But then again, she did want to please him, to keep him happy. It was her job, and she was a woman who took her job very seriously.

"I don't think that would be a good idea," she said softly, and before he could ask her why, she was gone.

* * *

Every Tuesday night, Cassandra wrote her mother a letter. It had become a habit, and she could not sleep on Tuesday nights until her letter was written. She always posted the letter from the office on Wednesday morning, and it was delivered on Thursday afternoon. Sometimes the letters were brief, if she was busy or if the week had been uneventful, but on other nights the letters were pages long.

These days e-mail made keeping in touch easy, and Cassandra did use that form of communication regularly. But her mother had told her how she loved receiving an old-fashioned handwritten letter now and then, and this tradition had been born. Now it was a ritual, one she didn't dare miss.

Dear Mum,
Lexie is off to Greece with Stanley. I suppose you already know that, but since Lexie is not the best of communicators I thought I'd pass the news along. She'll be gone a month.

Dressed in loose-fitting yellow pajamas, a cup of cooling tea at her elbow, Cassandra tapped the end of her pen against the pad of blue paper. The paper was unlined, and was decorated with a smattering of pink and lavender flowers along the left margin. The pad sat on her desk, and she perched on the edge of her chair. Should she mention the sheik or not? Her first instinct was *not,* but there would be no hiding the man if they took a tour of Barton College. Cassandra straightened her spine. And why on earth would she hide His Excellency, Sheik Kadir? She often wrote about her work, and the sheik was all about work. Nothing else.

I began a new and very exciting assignment today. A representative of the Kahani Foreign Ministry is visiting the country for the next three weeks, and I am to be his guide and aide for the duration. All those nights of studying Arabic have finally paid off. This is a plum assignment, and I'm happy to have it. You could say it's the chance I've been waiting for. Ms. Dunn, who is always so hard to please, said I had the qualifications necessary to fulfill this assignment.

The sheik is very well-known. The short version is His Excellency Sheik Kadir Al-Nuri. Perhaps you saw his picture in the newspaper. There was an article in the Silvershire Times about his impending visit, and I believe it ran three or four days ago.

Again she tapped the end of her pen against the paper. She could leave it at that but her mother was practically psychic, in that way only mothers can be. She seemed to know things she should not, and this short letter might illicit a "what aren't you telling me?" response. It was so unfair.

We will likely be taking a tour of the college. That was Al-Nuri's suggestion, not mine. I never would've thought he'd be interested. He has ideas of founding a women's college much like Barton in his own country, which is quite ambitious if you remember how archaic some of their customs are.

He wants to make changes, and I suppose I must admire him for that. In any case, the sheik and I will probably be there sometime in the next three weeks. I'm not sure when. I'll have to tinker with the schedule. Perhaps we'll see you while we're there.

Cassandra wasn't about to tell her mother that Al-Nuri had actually asked if he could meet her during the tour of Barton. That request sounded so personal, and it would certainly raise questions she didn't want to answer. She started to sign off, but thought better of it. Perhaps she should end the letter on a more personal note.

I think I ate some bad salad dressing at lunch today, but tonight all is well.
Love,
Cassandra

She sealed the letter in an envelope that matched the notepaper, and placed it beside her purse so she wouldn't forget it in the morning. That done, she dumped out the half-empty teacup, brushed her teeth, turned out the lights and crawled into the waiting bed.

Her mother had always called her Cassandra, but almost everyone else was determined to shorten her name to Cassie or Cass. After a while, it sounded petulant to insist that they call her by her full name, so she simply accepted whatever they wished to call her. Her sisters called her Cass, and always had. Even her dad called her Cass, and she really didn't mind. Coming from her family the name sounded fitting enough. When people she'd just met immediately shortened her name, it annoyed her.

Al-Nuri had asked if he could call her Cassandra. Not Cass, not Cassie…Cassandra. The way he said her name, the way the word rolled so sensually off his tongue as if he could taste it… Heaven above, the man could be trouble. If she allowed him to be, that is. And she would not.

She pulled the covers to her chin, then closed her eyes and insisted that sleep come quickly and deeply. Right before she drifted off, she whispered the fervent hope that she not dream of bedroom eyes and slightly accented *Cassandras*.

Chapter 3

The museum was only mildly interesting. The building itself was large and modern, not at all in keeping with the rest of the city. There was lots of glass and sharp lines that did not mesh well with the older, more quaint sections of the city. Large rooms that connected like a twisted maze were filled with paintings and drawings, intricate carvings and displays of ancient weaponry that had some significance to Silvershire history.

As much as Kadir admired fine art, no painting or sculpture could hold a candle to his personal tour guide, the lovely Ms. Klein. Once again she had dressed in a plain and conservative suit, and her pale hair was pulled back severely. Today, however, he occasionally caught her in a blush, and there was a light in her eyes she could not disguise, no matter how she tried. Like it or not, she was affected by his presence.

As he was affected by hers.

She was a wealth of information, telling him something about each artist and each artifact. Soon her words began to run together, and he simply watched and enjoyed her. Every display in the museum dulled beside her beauty, and he did not feel guilty to enjoy watching her instead of the artworks he was meant to appreciate.

Photographers were awaiting their departure from the museum, alerted to his presence by a museum employee, no doubt. Kadir was accustomed to camera flash bulbs and unflattering photographs plastered in newspapers around the world. In truth, no part of his life was his own—and so he smiled for the cameras as he strode along the paved path, and waved when his name was called. Ms. Klein held back, allowing him and his guards to be the focus of the photographs. Too bad, since a picture of her would be much more pleasant than one of his own.

Fahd and Jibril were tense. Yesterday's assassination attempt, which they had managed to keep out of the press, had them on edge. Rightfully so. This trip to Silvershire had been well publicized in the past few weeks, so Zahid surely knew where Kadir was. Would Bin-Asfour be bold enough to make an attempt here, in another country, or would he wait for Kadir to return to his home before trying again?

As they reached the parking lot—Fahd and Jibril alert, Hakim and Tarif lagging behind, and Ms. Klein doing her best to hide—a photographer made his way past the barricade and moved in for a closer shot. He lifted his camera and took a series of photographs before Jibril rushed to the photographer and forced the man back to his proper place.

Jibril was a large man, so it was unexpected that the

smallish photographer would put up a fight. He did, however, and Fahd did his best to hurry Kadir to the waiting limousine, which was bulletproof and could move very, very fast when necessary. As Kadir increased his step in order to accommodate his bodyguard, the unmistakable sound of a gunshot reverberated through the humid air.

Kadir spun away from Fahd and away from the limousine, instinctively grabbing Ms. Klein's arm. He pulled her to him, protected her as best he could with his body and threw them both toward the opened car door and safety. Behind them onlookers and photographers shouted and fell to the ground, and Jibril shouted orders in crisp Arabic. Ms. Klein screamed as they vaulted through the air and into the back seat of the limousine, where he landed on top of her. Fahd slammed the door shut, but as no more gunshots reverberated, Kadir deduced that the immediate danger was over.

Two attempts on his life in two days, and all he could think about was the softness of the woman beneath him.

Her cheeks reddened, and her lush lips parted slightly. One of her slender legs was caught between his, in an awkward and yet somehow apt position, and she'd instinctively wrapped her arms around him. Though they were no longer vaulting through the air, she did not loosen her hold. Her heart beat so hard and fast he could feel it, pounding against his own.

"Are you unharmed?" he asked, his voice low.

"Yes." The single word trembled. "You?"

"I'm fine." They had moments—mere seconds, perhaps—before they were joined by the rest of the party.

And still, Kadir did not move. The body beneath his fit very nicely, and no suit, no matter how severe, could disguise the softness he felt. Cassandra Klein was very much a woman, and he did not want to move. Not yet.

"Perhaps you should…get off of me," she suggested, not as forcefully as she could have.

"Perhaps I should." And still he didn't.

She was so close, and so tempting. It would be very easy to lay his lips over hers. There wasn't time for a true, deep kiss, but even a quick brushing of his lips against hers would be delicious. It was entirely inappropriate to kiss one's diplomatic aide. Even to think about taking such an action was improper. And yet he did think….

Outside the car, his bodyguards shouted to one another in Arabic, and bystanders yelled in excited English. The commotion seemed rather distant and was easily dismissed from his mind. Kadir watched the intriguing parting of lush lips just inches from his own, saw the flash of passion in dove-gray eyes and thought of more pleasant days. And more pleasant days to come, perhaps?

"Now may I call you Cassandra?"

She opened her mouth to say no. He could see and feel the no coming, just as clearly as he had seen her desire. In her eyes, on those lips…the no was right there. And then she hesitated.

"Perhaps when we are alone you can call me by my given name," she said. "There's nothing wrong with that, I suppose. Of course, we shouldn't be alone," she added in a quicker voice. "Between your bodyguards and assistants and the press and the staff at the estate and—"

As if to prove her point, the car door opened swiftly. "The shooter escaped, Excellency." Jibril very neatly ignored the compromising position in which he found his employer. "Fahd tried to give chase, but when it became clear the would-be assassin was gone, he returned."

Kadir sat up slowly, and Ms. Klein—Cassandra—followed. She tried to straighten her mussed hair, but flying through the air and landing in the back seat of the car beneath him had undone the severity, and he suspected it could not be easily repaired. Her skirt had ridden up her leg, and the hem sat nicely high on her thigh, a pleasant diversion she quickly remedied.

Hakim and Tarif gratefully scrambled into the safety of the limousine, both visibly shaken. Neither of them had ever been in the military, and at the moment it showed. They were scared, and would not easily shake off the morning's excitement.

"The duke has top-notch security personnel at hand, and they will begin investigating the shooting immediately," Cassandra said in a purely business voice, as if she had not just been beneath him, as if she had not been inches from a kiss.

"That is not necessary," Kadir said calmly.

"What do you mean it's not necessary?" she asked, her voice almost sharp. "Someone took a shot at you, and you might've been killed. That is unacceptable."

"No investigation is necessary, as I know full well who ordered that shot."

Again she tried to straighten her hair. Again she failed.

"Zahid Bin-Asfour," he continued. "I doubt he fired the weapon himself, but he surely ordered it done."

"Terrorists will not be allowed a presence in Silvershire," Cassandra said, as if her words alone could stop them.

Kadir leaned back against the seat as the car sped away from the museum. "That sounds very logical, but there is no logic in terrorism. Zahid took an old and precious ideal of tribe and unity and love of ancient culture, he took the concept of brotherhood and twisted it into a thing of hate and bloodshed. In the name of taking the people he claims to love back to a simpler yet harsher time, he is willing to kill anyone who disagrees with him. He wraps his own twisted need for power in words of heritage and dignity, and then he destroys both in violence and hate. Zahid Bin-Asfour is a criminal. A murderer and a drug dealer. There is no logic in his reasoning, Ms. Klein."

"I'm sure you're right, b-but…" She stammered, and blushed again. He was quite sure this woman never stammered.

Kadir leaned closer to Cassandra and whispered, "Ah, you are worried about me?"

"No!" she answered quickly. Then she retracted her denial. "I mean, of course as your escort your safety is my responsibility. I'll order a new guard to add to your own, and adjust the schedule," she said. "From now on no one will know of our planned activities in advance."

"No additional guards," Kadir said in a soft voice that left no room for argument.

"But…"

"No more."

Cassandra took a deep breath and said nothing, but he expected she'd argue for an increased guard again. And soon. He would refuse again. While he was not foolish enough to ignore security concerns, he would not hide behind an army—not Kahani's, and certainly not Silvershire's.

He should promise her, and himself, that he would not behave so inappropriately again, that he would not think of kissing her—and more. He should vow to keep their relationship professional and distant, as was right and proper.

But he didn't.

* * *

Her heart continued to pound because someone had shot at her. At least, that's what Cassandra tried to tell herself, even though the shooting had taken place hours ago.

Al-Nuri and his entourage were back at the estate they called home for the time being, and she was waiting for Ms. Dunn to finish with an important phone call so she could have a word. Sheik Kadir didn't want extra security, but he was going to get it anyway. If anything happened to him while he was in her care… If anything happened to him *at all*…

Cassandra was called into Ms. Dunn's office, after waiting almost half an hour. She was so wound up, she began talking as she walked through the door and toward the older woman's desk. "His Excellency Sheik Kadir is most anxious for a meeting with Lord Carrington. I understand that the timing is not best for Lord Carrington, but surely something can be arranged in a timely manner."

Ms. Dunn leaned back in her large leather chair—all ninety pounds or so of her dominating the room in an eerie but unmistakable way. "Take a deep breath and relax, Cassie. The meeting Sheik Kadir desires will take place in due time, most likely."

Ms. Dunn indicated that she could sit, but sitting was impossible when her heart was pounding this way and she could feel the blood rushing through her veins. Cassandra stood at the end of the wide walnut desk. "What do you mean, most likely?"

Assistant director for the Ministry of Foreign Affairs, a woman who had been in foreign service for more than forty years, Nola Dunn was an imposing figure. Cassandra had never spoken sharply to her before. It had probably been years since anyone had dared to say much more than "Yes, ma'am."

Ms. Dunn did not seem annoyed by Cassandra's brazenness. "When I gave you this assignment, I informed you that Prince Reginald met with Zahid Bin-Asfour shortly before his death."

"Yes, ma'am, I recall that very well." It was for that very reason that the terrorist was suspected in the prince's murder.

"And you are also aware that Bin-Asfour and the government of Kahani are all but at war, and have been for a very long time."

"Yes, ma'am."

Ms. Dunn placed thin arms on her desk and leaned forward. "What if Bin-Asfour isn't responsible for the assassination of Prince Reginald? What if he and Reginald were working together, and the government of Kahani is behind the murder?"

"But..."

"Until we know with certainty that Kahani is in no way involved in the prince's assassination, there can be no meeting between the Duke and your sheik. It has the potential to be a public relations nightmare. At the same time, we can't treat Al-Nuri as if he or his country is suspect in the matter, not when all we have is a theory. Keep him happy. Promise him the meeting he desires will take place when the time is right. And keep him far, far away from the palace. Is that clear?"

Cassandra knew, without a doubt, that Al-Nuri was in no way involved in Prince Reginald's murder. Even if his government had a hand in the assassination, *he* would not be involved. He was too good. Too kind and well-meaning. That was an argument she could not put forth at this time. Not without proof.

So she asked, "Why would Prince Reginald align himself with a terrorist?"

Ms. Dunn waved a bony hand. "It's just a supposition, and an unlikely one at that. But until we know more, it's best that Al-Nuri be kept a safe distance from the palace. And Lord Carrington."

"Yes, ma'am."

Ms. Dunn studied Cassandra up and down, her eyes cautious. "You were the target of a shooting today."

"Al-Nuri was the target," Cassandra corrected. There was quite a bit of difference, in her mind.

"Still, you were there. I'm sure it was a harrowing experience."

"It was..." She thought about the confusion that had followed the gunshot; the way Al-Nuri had grabbed her with strong arms; the slamming of the car door that had separated them from the melee; the weight of his body on hers, and the way he had looked at her with those bedroom eyes. "It was distressing, that's true, but the entire episode was soon over and no one was harmed."

Ms. Dunn's eyes actually twinkled. "I have great hopes for you, Cassie. You're a tough girl, and you're very smart. One day you could very well find yourself in this chair. For now I'm glad to have you on my team."

Cassandra wanted to tell her superior that she preferred "Cassandra" to "Cassie," and "woman" to "girl," but she'd likely pushed her limits enough for one day.

Ms. Dunn neatly changed the subject. "The king had surgery earlier today. The tumor was removed, and the physician says the procedure was a success."

It was privileged news, though likely not for long. "So he'll recover?"

Ms. Dunn shrugged, but it was not a casual, uncaring gesture. "It's too soon to tell. He remains in a coma."

Cassandra wondered if there was a hidden message in Ms. Dunn's bit of gossip. The future of the country was more important than the wishes of one man. In such uncertain times, any detail might be crucial—including keeping Al-Nuri and Lord Carrington separated until they knew more. She turned to leave the room, wondering how she'd keep Al-Nuri occupied for the duration of his stay. He was determined to have his meeting, and she couldn't arrange it for him. Not yet, at least.

Ms. Dunn had told Cassandra she could one day be in that chair. It was everything she had ever hoped for. For the first time she reached deep and asked herself: Was that really what she wanted? Did she want to be like Nola Dunn? Powerful, intelligent, very much in the inner circle.

And also very much alone.

"Cassie," Ms. Dunn called.

At the doorway, Cassandra turned. Oddly enough, the usually sour old woman was smiling. It was quite disconcerting.

"Mind yourself. Al-Nuri is a handsome devil and can be a womanizer, from what I hear. I wouldn't have given you this assignment if I didn't think you could handle him."

"I appreciate the confidence, ma'am."

Ms. Dunn waved a hand in dismissal. "Just be careful."

Cassandra nodded, quite sure the warning had nothing to do with bullets and assassination attempts.

* * *

Late Thursday morning, Kadir received a short but informative phone call from Sharif. Mukhtar's family had been rescued, and in the process a number of Zahid's recruits had been killed. Two of the soldiers with Sharif had been wounded, but there had been no loss of life on that side of the fight. The terrorists were well settled into the series of old buildings, making it clear that Zahid was trying to reestablish himself in Kahani. No wonder he'd attempted to kill Kadir. No one would fight Bin-Asfour and his ambitions harder—except perhaps Sharif.

Kadir had been hoping that perhaps Zahid would be there when the raid took place, or that one of his men would give up information on his whereabouts. Neither of those hopes came true.

On Thursday afternoon, the lovely Cassandra Klein took him on a tour of well-tended private gardens at an estate north of the capital city of Silverton. They were pretty but unexciting, and Kadir could not get the important matters that ruled his life out of his head. Zahid Bin-Asfour. The meeting with Lord Carrington. Mukhtar's violent end. The shooting at the museum, just yesterday morning. It was difficult to become excited about a rare flower when such events crowded his mind.

Fahd and Jibril had placed themselves on opposite ends of the neat garden Kadir and Cassandra explored, ready to defend their charge if necessary, but also lulled by the quiet and serenity of the well-manicured grounds.

Kadir stopped in the middle of the neat pathway and turned to face Cassandra. Now this was a sight that could clear all unpleasantness from his mind. He saw no imperfections on her face, no flaw on her carefully and conservatively clad body. There was a spark of passion in her eyes, as he had noted often in the past two days. Was there a man in her life who awakened that passion?

"Do you have a man in your life?"

She was so startled by his question, she actually twitched. "My personal life is really none of your business, Excellency."

"I'm simply curious," he responded. "A husband, a suitor, an affianced one…"

"No," she answered curtly, blushing slightly. "I'm a single woman. My career is very important to me, and that leaves little time for…for…"

"Romance?" Kadir supplied.

"Whatever. Now, that's all I intend to say on the subject of my personal life."

That suited Kadir, since the fact that she was unattached was all he needed to know. He gladly changed the subject. "Do you like this sort of garden, Cassandra?"

She was startled by his use of her name, but a quick look around assured her that they were—for all intents and purposes—alone. "What do you mean? It's just a garden. A very nice garden, of course. Aren't all gardens of the same sort?"

He smiled, and again she blushed. "No, all gardens are not of the same sort. Not at all. Personally, I prefer a garden where the plants are allowed to grow wild, where to make your way along the path you must push around and beyond untamed growth. I prefer large blooms that are red and bright yellow and deep purple, bright colors that remind us that life is beautiful." He studied the pastel flowers along the methodical path. "It takes a sturdy plant to survive that sort of gardening. These pale blooms would not survive in such a garden. They would be choked out by the brighter blooms that dare to reach for the sun. Their thin roots would be overtaken by thick, healthy roots that reach for nutrients and claim the soil with a vengeance." He glanced down to find Cassandra studying him with wide, curious eyes. "A wild life is not suitable for something too delicate."

It occurred to him, as he finished, that he wasn't talking about gardens anymore. In the past his life had been wild and untamed. On some days it was still bright, but he'd become so entrenched in his job, so dedicated to his mission, that the colors had dulled somewhat. Dulled, but not entirely faded.

The danger to his life was very real, and while he could and did take all proper precautions, there was no way to make his life entirely safe. Cassandra Klein was a pale and delicate flower that would not survive in such terrain.

And, of course, she would never be called upon to try.

He wanted, very much, to kiss her. The desire to do so was improper, imprudent. It was definitely foolish. And yet, he did want a kiss. Maybe if he laid his lips over hers and took a proper kiss, he would taste the wildflower in her soul. Perhaps she was not as delicate as she appeared to be.

"I'm sorry you're not enjoying the outing," Cassandra said, her voice all business once again. "I can see that these gardens are not of interest to you. Tomorrow we'll…"

"Barton College tomorrow," he said with a smile, not bothering to tell her that certain gardens were very much of interest.

"But…"

"You said we would vary our schedule so no one would know where to find us. I wish to see Barton College tomorrow."

Her shoulders squared. “All right. If that’s what you wish.”

He leaned slightly toward her. “And I will meet your mother?”

Cassandra sighed and glanced away. “I suppose you will.”

“Good. We’ll leave early, and I’ll drive.”

“But…”

“I’ll drive,” he said again.

Kadir took Cassandra’s arm and led her down the well-manicured garden path, the scent of summer blooms filling the air, wondering as he walked toward Jibril how he would manage to separate himself from the dedicated security staff that was determined to protect him twenty-four hours a day. He was tired of the order of his own life. Tired of the dullness that had taken hold.

He longed to be a wildflower himself again, just for a while.

Chapter 4

Cassandra closed her eyes and tried to keep her stomach from completely leaving her body. Once again the sheik was messing with her insides, only this time it was his driving skills that had her feeling light-headed. She had never traveled this familiar road so *fast*.

She opened one eye and glanced at Al-Nuri. The man smiled widely, enjoying this insane trip. With the wind in his shoulder-length hair, sunglasses hiding those sinful bedroom eyes and wearing clothing much more casual than he normally wore, he looked like a different man.

He turned his head to her and the grin grew even wider. Oh, no, he truly was insane.

"Watch the road!" she commanded.

He did as she instructed, and she closed her eyes again.

Al-Nuri had very sleekly ditched his bodyguards this morning, leaving poor Tarif with a tale to tell—a tale of a long day of important phone calls that could not be interrupted, a tale of boring diplomatic work that required a full day alone in the estate office the sheik called his own for this trip. That done, Al-Nuri had slipped into Prentiss Redmond's garage and appropriated a small black convertible—with Oscar's assistance, of course.

At this rate they'd arrive at Barton College in half the time it usually took Cassandra to make the trip.

This road was a fairly good one, but it was in need of repair here and there, and it twisted and turned along a few stretches. Al-Nuri didn't even slow down for the sharpest of curves, and the slightest bump took them airborne.

Heaven above, he was going to kill her. She was going to die a virgin, without knowing the love she'd waited for *or* the meaningless sex Lexie recommended. At this rate she'd never know the joy of being an almost-psychic mother, like her own mum. She was going to die in a perfectly acceptable but definitely dreary navy blue suit, with her hair tangled and hopelessly mussed by the wind that had undone her French braid long ago.

The car whipped around, jerking the very breath out of her, and came to a sudden stop. Cassandra very cautiously opened her eyes. Al-Nuri had pulled the car to the side of the road. Just ahead was a sign that read Barton 8 kms.

She glared at him. "You were speeding."

He was so obviously enjoying himself, she couldn't remain angry. "I know," he said. "It was marvelous."

She didn't want to smile, but how could she help herself? Sheik Kadir, His Excellency, looked like a ten-year-old boy who had just discovered the joys of the roller coaster. There was such delight on his very masculine face. "Why did we stop?"

To her surprise, he leaned across the console, cupped her head in his large hand and pulled her mouth to his. Slowly, and yet with urgency. That hand was firm but gentle, and she had time to pull away when she realized what he was about to do. She didn't.

He kissed her. Deeply, completely and with the same joy with which he had driven this borrowed sports car, he kissed her. She kissed him back, even though it was entirely inappropriate and unexpected and wrong. This time her stomach did more than flutter. It clenched, leapt and danced. So did her heart. The tip of his tongue just barely teased her bottom lip, and she felt something powerful climb into her throat. A moan. A demand.

Something she had to drive down and ignore.

Cassandra drew away, confused by her intense reaction. She should be stronger than this. She knew better. *He* knew better! "Excellency, I have known you three days."

"I know." One masculine hand brushed away a wild strand of blond hair that teased her cheek. "Three days is a long time to wait for a kiss, but..."

"No, it has not been a *long time,*" she said sternly. "The point is, I barely know you!"

He was not chastened, that she could tell. "You sound disapproving, and yet you did not kiss in that way. Should I believe my ears, or my mouth?"

"Believe whatever you want. Just don't do that again."

He pulled back into the driver's seat and studied her. She could not see his eyes behind those dark glasses to judge his reaction. "If I misread your interest, then I apologize."

"Apology accepted, Excellency," she said.

He sighed. "I thought you might call me Kadir when we are alone."

"You thought wrong." *About a lot of things.*

Al-Nuri drove the rest of the way more sedately, and he kept his eyes on the road. The wide smile that had been so oddly enchanting was gone now, and that was for the best. She knew he was a playboy of sorts. Did he always seduce his female aides for his own pleasure and entertainment? Did he keep notches in his headboard? Were there broken hearts spread all around the world?

Fluttering stomach or no, she would not be made a fool by a man whose only interest was a bedmate for his three-week stay. Two and a half weeks left, she noted, as she mentally counted down the days.

Barton College was an old and prestigious campus, and the grounds were well kept. They were not as annoyingly tidy as the manicured garden he had visited yesterday, but still the grounds were neat. There were old trees and precisely trimmed hedges on soft green hills, and the buildings that made up the campus were constructed of sturdy gray stone that looked cold even beneath the early-afternoon sun, which shone down brightly.

Kadir had met the dean—a stern and intelligent middle-aged woman—and he'd spoken with several students. A few of the students had giggled in an annoying and inexplicable manner, but they were very young and silly, so he'd dismissed their inappropriate behavior.

He had more important things on his mind.

He'd been planning to move to his yacht this weekend, at least for a few days. It was clear that Lord Carrington had no intention of agreeing anytime soon to the meeting Kadir had requested, and Kadir had no desire to play tourist for the next two weeks, before the gala he had come here to attend was held. The yacht was anchored near the north shore town of Leonia, in the quiet Leonia Bay, and a few days of peace in a place he could truly call his own would be welcomed.

But moving onto the yacht so far away from Silverton would surely mean leaving his assigned aide behind, and he was not ready to walk away from Cassandra Klein. She intrigued him in a way no woman ever had.

Cassandra had been unusually silent during the tour of the college. Not just silent, but subdued. Withdrawn. It was the kiss that had done it, he knew. Even though she had enjoyed the kiss and had participated fully, it continued to disturb her. It was easy enough for Kadir to decipher the true reason for her mood.

They walked along a shaded path that led to a small park that overlooked the Lodan River. He found an empty bench and sat, leaving room for Cassandra beside him. She chose instead to stand behind the wooden bench, rigid and unforgiving.

He patted the seat beside him with patient fingers.

"No, thank you," she answered softly.

"I won't bite," he said. "Or kiss." He waited a moment, and she didn't move. "Please," he added in a lowered voice.

Eventually Cassandra rounded the bench and sat beside him—if you could call perching at the far opposite end of the bench "beside." She'd been forced to take her hair down, since the brisk ride in Redmond's convertible had mussed her hair so that there was nothing to be done but let it down and brush it out. He had not realized her hair was so long. It was always tightly restrained, which he could now see was a true crime.

"I don't normally kiss diplomatic aides," he began.

She scoffed.

"Actually, I have never kissed a diplomatic aide before today. It's unprofessional and potentially messy."

"Exactly," she said, obviously relieved. Apparently she had mistaken his comment to mean that he agreed with her. He did not.

"But you, Cassandra, you are different."

Her head snapped around, and soft, pale hair danced. "I am *not* different," she argued. "And you can't expect me to believe..." Her sentence trailed off, but he understood her meaning. How odd, that he could look at her face and know what she was thinking. It had been years since he'd felt so deeply connected to any person. And a woman he wanted to sleep with? Never.

"It has been a very long time since I wanted anything for myself," he said. "Years. So many years, I can't even say how many." Well, he could, but he wouldn't. There would be time for that later, perhaps. "I have been caught up in my purpose, my career, my mission, until there is nothing else in my world. You make me want something else. From the moment I saw you—"

"Stop," she commanded. "Excellency, this is..."

"Kadir."

She turned her head to glare at him. "*Excellency,* I am not the kind of woman you obviously think I am."

"I think you are beautiful and intelligent and kind. Am I wrong?"

Her lips pursed slightly. "I'm not the kind of woman who can give a man...something else." She blushed. "Anything else. My career is very important to me, Excellency. I won't do anything to tarnish it."

Sleeping with him would definitely tarnish her reputation. And his. If they were caught, that is. He was not blind to the fact that they had no future. Her life was here in Silvershire. His was in Kahani, and as Kahani's representative around the world. They were too dissimilar to even think of anything beyond the span of his visit in her country, but did that mean they had to deny what they both so obviously felt?

"Your career is more important than the excitement and the beauty of life?" he asked. "More important than joy?" More important than love? He would not put that question to her, since he had not known her long enough to speak the word *love.* He would not promise—or even hint at—anything he could not offer.

"My career is the most important thing in my life," she explained, and her eyes begged him not to make the coming days difficult for her. "In truth, it's the only important thing in my life. Don't misunderstand, I love my sisters and my parents, and I have friends. But I've dedicated myself to my career to the exclusion of everything else. Yesterday you asked about my personal life, and I made it very clear that I don't have one. I don't have time for anything beyond my career. One day, perhaps, but not now." She appeared flustered, and more uncertain than she wished to be. "I can't allow you to come in here and ruin everything I've worked for."

Kadir sighed. There was nothing he could say to make Cassandra understand that his interest in her wasn't entirely casual. They had no future—that was true enough—but still…she was special. Different. There was no way he could sit here and make her understand that he couldn't replace her with another woman and be just as happy if that woman welcomed his attentions.

He wanted her. No one else would do. And judging

by the expression on her face, he was not going to have her. He could try to change her mind, if the opportunity arose, but he could not—would not—push her into a temporary relationship that she obviously didn't want.

A pair of students walked by. One carried a sloppily folded newspaper. They both tittered.

Kadir was suddenly easily annoyed. "What is wrong with these idiotic, snickering students?"

Cassandra purposely saved the visit to the art department for last. The least amount of time Al-Nuri and Piper Klein spent together, the better off they'd all be. Hello, goodbye, we're back on the road again.

Oh, she did not look forward to the return trip.

"Cassandra!" Piper rushed forward, leaving behind her desk piled high with books and papers. "I was just about to go out and hunt you down. I heard hours ago that you were on campus."

With a smile Cassandra said, "I was saving the best for last, of course."

Piper turned calculating and approving eyes on Al-Nuri. "You must be the sheik." She offered her hand. "Piper Klein. Pleased to meet you."

Cassandra took a deep, calming breath. "Mum, you're to address him as Excellency. That's what's proper."

Al-Nuri turned on his most brilliant smile as he took Piper's hand. "Don't be proper on my account. I have told your daughter many times that I care little for what is proper." He continued to hold her hand. "Call me Kadir, please."

Oh, no, no, please don't, Cassandra thought.

"Kadir," Piper said. "What a lovely name."

So much for almost-psychic Mum.

Piper Klein was fifty-six years old, still trim and still pretty. She had lively blue eyes and a sense of adventure, and usually had paint or clay—or both—under her fingernails. Cassandra had gotten her gray eyes from her Dad, but everything else in the gene pool came straight from her mother. She had missed the sense of adventure, however, which was just as well. That sense of adventure hadn't done Lexie any good at all.

For a few long minutes, Piper regaled Al-Nuri with tales of her years at Barton College. Cassandra listened closely. If her mother ventured into "When Cassandra was a baby..." territory, this visit was *over.* But their conversation remained all about the college, and about Al-Nuri's plans to fund one much like it in Kahani.

He was a man like all others in many ways—the kiss had proven that point—but in many ways he was unique. He did want to change the world for the better. He wanted to make a difference in a country where a college like this one would affect countless lives.

She wouldn't kiss him again, but that didn't mean she couldn't admire him, as a man and as a politician.

Cassandra knew she would probably never forget that kiss, and though she would never let Al-Nuri or anyone else know...she wanted another one. Strictly as an experiment, of course. Would another kiss be as wonderfully alarming? Would it make her heart do strange things? She might be a virgin, but she *had* kissed men before.

None had ever kissed her the way Al-Nuri did, sinfully and with a delicious completeness. None of those previous kisses had made her want more than she could have. Surely her reaction to his kiss was an aberration, and another would prove that he was no different from any other man.

The dean arrived with a folder of papers that contained some details about finances and curriculum for Al-Nuri, and the sheik wandered in her direction. Piper took that moment to scurry over to her daughter.

"Oh, my goodness," she whispered. "He's amazing. Handsome, rich, powerful and *nice.*" Piper waved a dismissive hand. "I'm sure he has qualities that are less than wonderful—all men do—but what I have seen so far is absolutely perfect." She smiled widely. "You were right to wait for a man like this one to come along."

Cassandra's expression didn't change. "I have no idea what you're talking about."

Almost-psychic Mum's answer was a gentle slap on the arm. "Don't be embarrassed. Bad salad dressing, indeed. Even if you hadn't told me, I still would've figured it out on my own."

"I didn't tell you anything," Cassandra argued, her voice low.

"You told me everything I need to know in your letter, though I did have to see beyond your little code. He's marvelous, he's smart, I ate bad salad dressing."

"I think it was rancid."

Piper snorted. "Besides, I saw the picture. Did you think I wouldn't?"

Cassandra cocked her head to one side and blinked, confused. What on earth was her mum talking about? "What picture?"

"Isn't it a little late for playing innocent, Cassandra? Really, a man doesn't go to such measures unless he feels *something.* It's very gallant and romantic, and…"

Piper narrowed her eyes as she studied her youngest daughter's puzzled eyes. "Oh, dear, you really haven't seen it, have you?"

It was the expression on her mother's face that caused Cassandra's wave of sick dread. "Haven't seen what?"

Piper rushed to her desk, and Cassandra followed closely. A quick glance back showed her that Al-Nuri was keeping the dean entertained for the moment. At the messy desk, Piper moved a stack of books aside and grabbed a newspaper.

One quick glance, and Cassandra knew what newspaper it was. "Mother! You read that trash?" The *Silvershire Inquisitor* was nothing more than a tawdry gossip tabloid. The *Quiz,* as it was called by most, was certainly not fit for Barton College's esteemed art professor.

Piper folded the paper so the top half of the front page was revealed. The logo of an eye—all-seeing, apparently—dominated. But just beneath that eye was a photograph that grabbed Cassandra's attention and held on.

It was her. And Al-Nuri. Well, it was their legs, more specifically. Entangled and extended from the back seat of the limo, moments after he'd grabbed her and thrown her toward safety.

Al-Nuri's legs were covered by his dark trousers. Since her skirt was riding high on her thighs, her legs were very much bare. And rather…spread, so that he was, for that second in time, between them. Beneath the photo, in bold type, words screamed, Sensational Sheik Saves Sexy Secretary!

"I am not a secretary!" Cassandra protested.

"Don't take it personally, dear. I'm sure the word choice was strictly for the alliteration."

Beneath the photo, on the bottom fold of the front page, there were two less sensational photos. One head shot of her, and one of Al-Nuri. No wonder the students had been giggling all day.

A quick glance at the article did nothing to ease her dread. Apparently the *sensational sheik* had thrown himself in front of a bullet in order to save her. There had been one bullet, and it had been intended for *him,* not her. Why did they have to make him out to be a hero? Later in the article, there was a not-so-subtle hint that perhaps Al-Nuri and the diplomatic aide he risked his life for were "involved." "Stay tuned for more juicy details," the author of the article promised.

All her care about sacrificing for her career, and this is where it got her. If people believed she and the sheik were improperly involved, it was just as bad—well, almost as bad—as if they really were....

Stealing kisses. Sharing personal confessions. Starting to like one another in a very undiplomatic way.

"What's this?"

That deep voice at her shoulder startled her, and she tried to crumple the paper in her hands. Al-Nuri reached out and took the *Quiz* from her, unfolding it slowly until the horrible photo was fully revealed.

"I'm going to sue," she said in a calm voice.

"Why? It's a very good photograph."

"It is not!"

He cocked his head to one side, as if he could see more that way.

"You were there, Excellency," Cassandra said. "There's no need to study the photo so closely."

"I did not see the incident from this angle," Al-Nuri said as he continued to peruse the photograph.

She tried to take it from him, but he was taller and stronger—and he managed to hold the newspaper out of her reach. Maybe it was foolish, but looking at that photo reminded her of how she'd felt at that moment. Not when he'd tossed her into the car, but just after, when his weight had been on her body and his lips had been so close....

"Please give me that paper, Excellency."

"I'm not finished."

"Yes, you are."

"I have not read the article."

Her heart leaped in pure dread. "Since half of it is untrue, there's no need, Excellency."

He looked down at her and smiled. The man had such a wicked grin. "Call me Kadir, and it is yours."

She hesitated, and he turned his attention to the article. The article in which he was a hero who'd saved her life, and they were lovers.

"Please give me the newspaper, *Kadir.*"

He stopped reading and looked her squarely in the eye. "Again."

"Kadir," she said, her voice softer.

It was enough to satisfy him, and he handed her the paper.

Kadir. It was a nice name, and it suited him much better than Excellency or Al-Nuri. She had suspected all along that simply calling him by his given name would make him feel too close. Too real. Too much like *hers.*

She'd been right.

Chapter 5

For the return trip, Al-Nuri had put the top up on the convertible. It looked as if they might run into a rain shower down the road, so it was a reasonable precaution. He also drove much more slowly, which was a relief.

Still, Cassandra missed his wicked, joyful smile. It was an unexpected response that she could not afford to indulge in. She never, ever, indulged in anything just for herself, or missed anything so inconsequential as a grin, or even considered placing her career second on her list of priorities. That had made perfect sense to her…until today. Suddenly she wasn't so sure her well-laid plans for the future were actually well-laid.

And wasn't that an unfortunate choice of words?

A few minutes more than half an hour from the college, the rain began. It didn't storm, but fat drops fell on and around the car. Al-Nuri turned on the windshield wipers and dropped his speed, since visibility on the winding road was not what it had once been. The radio was off, and they both remained silent. There was just the sound of rain and the wipers, swishing away at the intense quiet.

Cassandra turned her attention to the *Silvershire Inquisitor,* reading the front-page article about the museum shooting once again. The article was no less alarming than it had been the first time she'd read it.

"The story distresses you," Al-Nuri said in a lowered voice that sounded loud and ominous in the confines of the vehicle.

"Yes," she confessed as she turned to page two. "It should distress you, as well. We both have reputations to think of."

"You said the paper is not well-respected. Will anyone of importance give credence to the story?"

Cassandra sighed. "Probably not," she conceded. "But we will have to be very careful. There can't be any hint of impropriety between us."

Without warning, Al-Nuri pulled the car to the side of the road, put it in Park and then turned the key—silencing the engine and the wipers. For a long moment there was no sound other than the rain all around them. Raindrops fell on the canvas roof and the windshield, pattering softly. After a moment, Cassandra realized that she was holding her breath.

"Are you distressed because some unimportant person might believe you behaved inappropriately, or are you distressed because they might believe you're involved with an Arab from Kahani?"

Cassandra's head snapped up and around. "My annoyance with the *Quiz* has nothing to do with where you come from or who you are. I've worked very hard to get where I am within the Ministry of Foreign Affairs, and to have people think I use my position as an opportunity to—to hook up with men is insulting."

He seemed a bit relieved, but she couldn't be sure. "They will be watching us closely now, yes?"

"Yes. We can expect photographers to be waiting outside the estate, and if we want to go anywhere without them, we'll have to sneak out, as we did this morning. That won't be as easy as it was a few hours ago. The *Quiz* hadn't hit the stands when we left the estate."

Al-Nuri draped one arm across the steering wheel, in a casual—and yet not quite casual—pose. "Should I ask for another aide from your department for the duration of my visit?"

For a moment, Cassandra considered answering "Yes," but it didn't take long for her to reconsider. "No. I'm afraid that would only fuel the flames of the rumor. We must continue to work together as professionally as possible." Let the press take their pictures. Let them try to find something—anything—inappropriate.

"No one is watching us now," Al-Nuri said.

"No."

"This might be the last time we are truly alone."

She didn't like that idea, not at all. "I suppose so."

Al-Nuri didn't make a move, as he had on the breakneck trip to Barton College, but the way he looked at her...it was enough to make any woman's heart beat faster.

"Asking for one more kiss would surely be inappropriate," he said. "You've made it clear that you don't wish to become involved with me in any way other than professionally. I like you very much. I wish we had met under different circumstances, so I could pursue you with a clear conscience. But wishes are for children who still believe in dreams, not for grown men who are confronted each and every day with the harshness of reality. There are those who want me dead. I live surrounded by bodyguards because to ignore the danger would be foolish. And yet today I left that danger, that reality, behind, and I'm not sorry. I'm not ready for the day to end, Cassandra. I imagine you think I do this sort of thing all the time, but in that supposition you would be wrong. I admire you. I'm drawn to you. In a little more than two weeks I'll be gone, and your life will go on as it did before I arrived. You've made it clear that you don't wish anything to come of what we feel."

Cassandra thought of arguing that she felt *nothing,* but it would be a lie—and he'd know it.

"So, I wish for one more kiss," he said. "Here, where we are truly alone and no one will see. One last kiss, before reality returns. If the idea does not appeal to you on any level, say as much. Reject the idea and I will continue on, and will not mention it again. But if you feel, as I do, that such a kiss is necessary..."

Cassandra leaned slightly toward him. She'd liked it better when he'd just taken the kiss. Now he was making her choose, he was making her *think.* And she didn't want to think about this anymore.

One more kiss would prove to her that her reaction to the first one had been a fluke. One more kiss would remind her that Al-Nuri was no different than any other man. "Just kiss me, Kadir," she said. One more kiss to set her mind straight, and then she could dismiss the inappropriate feelings that grew stronger every time she looked at this man.

Al-Nuri—Kadir—placed his lips on hers, and as

before he cradled the back of her head in one large, warm hand. The kiss grew deeper quickly, and this time she tasted desperation as well as desire. She leaned closer, he held her tighter and her lips parted more widely. This was the last kiss—this was all they could have—and so she didn't want it to be over quickly. It had to last a while longer. His tongue danced gently with hers, and her arm snaked around his shoulder so she could hold on tight.

Sensations—passion, need, tenderness—all swelled inside her. It was as if her body pounded with what it wanted…what it needed. Like Kadir, she wished, for one impossible moment, that they had met under different circumstances.

But like him, she knew that was a foolish wish.

Had she really thought this kiss would remind her that he was just like any other man? He was not…and the kiss was truly extraordinary.

Cassandra drew away, breaking the kiss because she knew if she didn't, she'd soon be unable to stop. She was not a woman accustomed to losing control. Kadir dropped his head to her shoulder, and after a moment he laid his lips on the side of her neck. Briefly, warmly, tenderly and with emotion. He drew away slowly and looked her in the eye.

She hadn't eaten bad salad dressing for days, and yet…and yet…

Three photographers were waiting outside the Redmond Estate gates when Kadir and Cassandra returned, but as it was just after dark, the photographers couldn't tell who was in the vehicle. The sight of those photographers who had not been there that morning annoyed Kadir; it proved that Cassandra had been right, and in the coming weeks they must be very careful in the ways in which they presented themselves to the public.

Once they were inside the estate, Cassandra said a quick and obviously distracted farewell, and made her way to her own vehicle. She was anxious to escape. From the photographers and the article that disturbed her, and from him. He felt as if he were losing her as she drove away, though in truth she had never been his to lose.

Sayyid had discovered Kadir's escape late in the afternoon, but thanks to Tarif's and Oscar's explanations, the security guard was not overly concerned by the absence of his employer. Irked, yes, but not worried. No matter how annoyed he might be, Sayyid could say very little.

Kadir closed himself in his office and tried to attend to the business he had neglected all day. If he could arrange a meeting with Lord Carrington quickly, perhaps he should make an excuse for leaving before the gala took place. That meeting was his primary purpose for being in Silvershire, in any case, and his departure would certainly make Cassandra's life easier.

If he could do that for her, perhaps he should. She was not like the women who occasionally came in and out of his life, and there would be no opportunity for more to develop between them. It was best that he take care of the business that had brought him to Silvershire, and then leave, as quickly and quietly as possible.

Tomorrow morning he would call the Silvershire Ministry of Foreign Affairs and demand the meeting with Lord Carrington. Even on a Saturday morning, someone would be available to take his call.

It was getting late, and he was thinking of retiring for the evening, when Hakim knocked briefly, then opened the door and walked into the office with a brisk step. "You have a visitor, Excellency."

For a moment, Kadir wondered...Cassandra? But he knew it wouldn't be her, no matter how he wished it to be so.

"A Mr. Nikolas Donovan," Hakim finished.

"It's rather late. Can he wait until morning?"

Hakim's eyes were very tired. "I don't believe so, Excellency. He apparently waited for the photographers at the gate to leave, as he did not wish his visit to be recorded. Tomorrow morning the photographers may very well return."

The fact that Donovan didn't wish to be photographed entering the estate was intriguing. "Show him in."

Kadir knew, of course, who Nikolas Donovan was here to represent. He was well-informed of all the political factions in Silvershire, including the Union for Democracy.

Donovan had been searched for weapons, and still Sayyid insisted on being in the room during the meeting. As Kadir trusted the bodyguard with all his secrets—well, all of his *political* secrets—he didn't mind. The guard's presence did seem to distract Donovan at first, but Sayyid did his best to blend into the woodwork.

When introductions and cordial greetings had been made, Donovan took a seat on the opposite side of Kadir's desk.

"I'll get right to the point," Donovan said briskly. "You're well-respected in the diplomatic community, and I'm here to ask for your support for my cause."

"You want me to publicly support the Union for Democracy?" Kadir asked.

"Yes, Excellency," Donovan answered. "I believe we can be of some use to one another, if we align."

Aligning with the Union for Democracy would be in direct opposition to Kadir's planned affiliation with Lord Carrington. Though he personally admired what Donovan was trying to do, he could not condone that organization and still ask for an alliance with the monarchy of Silvershire. Besides, there were well-substantiated rumors that some factions within the Union for Democracy had begun to advocate violence as a way to meet their goals. Kadir was quite sure that Donovan was not among those who would turn to violence, but it was a chance he could not take.

"I'm afraid I must decline," Kadir answered without any softening of expression that might give away his personal feelings on the matter.

"Believe me, I understand that your position here is precarious. It's for that reason that I waited until the photographers left before calling. I don't want to put you in a difficult position. All I ask is that you consider my proposition."

Kadir shook his head. "I am here as a representative of my government in order to form an alliance with Lord Carrington, and as soon as I meet with him I'll return home."

"Good luck with that," Donovan said sharply. "Carrington has just left the country, and I don't believe he plans to return until a day or two before the Founder's Day Gala."

A small knot formed in Kadir's stomach. "Are you certain?"

"I met with him last night. He and his wife, Princess Amelia, were getting ready to leave for a visit to Gastonia."

Last night. Kadir sighed. Would nothing of his duties in this country proceed as they should?

"What do you think of Lord Carrington, Mr. Donovan? Will he make a good king?"

Donovan's jaw went tight and hard. "He's a decent man, a much better man than Prince Reginald."

Kadir smiled. "That isn't saying much, from what I hear of the departed prince."

"With the king in a coma, Carrington refuses to even discuss altering our antiquated system of government. The people should be able to decide who leads their country. I know that Kahani is also a monarchy, but you've been advocating change for years. What you and I want is not so very different."

"I'm not trying to overthrow a government."

"Neither am I," Donovan argued. "I want my country to advance into a new and more modern world, which is what you want for your country. Together we could advocate for that change in a much more powerful way than we can alone."

It was almost tempting, and there was something very likable about Donovan. He was intense, in that way visionaries often are. And yet—Kadir had no choice in the matter.

"Again, I must decline."

Donovan was disappointed, but not angry. It was a point in his favor that he didn't fly into a rage when he didn't get what he'd come here for. Of course, he was well aware that Sayyid watched his back, so perhaps he didn't dare lose his temper.

Business done, Donovan leaned back in his chair

and offered a gentle smile. "I saw your picture in the *Quiz* this morning."

Kadir lifted his eyebrows slightly. "Did you? I wouldn't think you'd waste your time reading such a disreputable newspaper."

"I never miss it. Between the stories of alien visitations and the adventures of dog boy, there's the occasional bit of truth that catches my eye."

Dog boy? Alien visitations?

Donovan's smile widened. "No one will admit they read the *Quiz,* but somehow everyone knows what's in it. It's one of our guilty pleasures, I suppose. Do you have guilty pleasures, Excellency?"

Not nearly enough. "If I did," Kadir said with a smile, "I would not admit as much to you."

"Of course not." Donovan stood, offering his hand across the desk.

Kadir rose and took that hand, shaking it firmly. "Good luck, Mr. Donovan."

"And to you, Excellency," Donovan answered. "If you change your mind, please contact me at your convenience. I'm easy enough to find. I believe you and I would work together well, given the chance."

Sayyid escorted Donovan from the room. When his visitor was gone, Kadir sat in his desk chair and leaned back, relaxing for a moment. Lord Carrington had left the country, so there would be no meeting in the near future. Why hadn't Cassandra told him Carrington was in Gastonia? Was it possible that she didn't know? Or was she keeping secrets from him?

In any case, it seemed there was no reason for him to remain here at the Redmond Estate. Tomorrow morning he would go to Leonia and take up residence on his yacht. Given the atmosphere following their trip to Barton College, Cassandra would probably be very happy to see him go.

Cassandra was just about to crawl into bed when the phone rang. The jangling noise startled her. Who would call so late? Was something wrong? Maybe it was Kadir, calling to say good-night.

She lifted the receiver from her bedside phone. "Hello?" she answered, her voice just slightly suspicious.

"I was hoping you wouldn't be asleep yet."

Cassandra breathed a sigh of relief at the sound of her mother's voice. "No, not yet. I'm headed in that direction, though."

After a short pause Piper asked, in a very soft voice, "Is he there?"

Cassandra didn't have to ask who *he* was. "No! Of course not! I told you, Mum, you have the wrong idea about what's going on here. Rather, what's *not* going on. My relationship with the sheik is entirely professional." At least, it was *now,* and would remain so for the duration of his visit. There would be no more kissing, no more conversations about dreams and wishes.

Piper sighed. "Too bad. I was rather hoping to have a sheik as a son-in-law one day. We could vacation in Kahani, which I hear is lovely. Would your sons be sheiks, too? I'm afraid I really don't know how that works. And Kadir really is a very nice man. I like him. And oh, my, he's so handsome. Are you sure he's not there?"

Cassandra couldn't help but laugh. "I'm sure."

"Too bad. It's long past time for you to take the plunge, Cassandra. You're smart not to fall for every line that's thrown your way, you're smart to wait for something more than out-of-control hormones." Again she sighed. "But really, darling, sometimes you're too smart. There comes a time when a woman has to follow her heart and forget what her head tells her. Love is a rare and precious thing, and if you allow love to pass you by without making a grab for it, it might never come again."

"What makes you think love has anything to do with this?" Cassandra tried to sound lighthearted, but she wasn't sure she succeeded.

"Because I know you," Piper answered confidently.

Cassandra reclined on the bed with the phone to her ear. "You're such a nosy mother," she said without anger. "All right. Since you're determined to pry where you should not, answer one question for me."

"Fire away."

Cassandra waited a moment before proceeding, and her mother remained silent. And then a dam burst and Cassandra began to talk rapidly. "How does a woman know if it's her heart speaking or her hormones? 'Out-of-control' hormones, you said. You know how I hate being out of control." A knot of uncertainty and unease formed very near to Cassandra's heart. "Is a man, any man, worth throwing away years of work and dedication and planning? How can a woman know if a man who speaks to her heart, or her hormones, cares for her in anything other than a physical way? And if you know a relationship can't possibly last, is it worth the pain of a potential heartbreak? Lexie was deliriously happy with each of her husbands and boyfriends, at least for a while. Would she have been better off turning her back on the good times to avoid the bad, or are the good times worth the pain that follows?"

Piper didn't answer immediately, and then she said slowly, "That's more than one question."

Frustrated, Cassandra said, "Well, pick one."

"All right." Piper took a deep breath. "Yes. The answer is yes."

"Which—"

"I have to go," Piper interrupted. "Your father's calling. I promised him a sandwich before bedtime."

"But—"

"Good night, darling. I love you."

The line went dead, and Cassandra was left holding a receiver. She stared at the receiver for a moment, as if that stare might bring her mother back. She needed real concrete answers to her questions, not a simple, single and nonspecific word. Soon there was a soft click, and the sound of a dial tone took the place of her mother's voice.

Cassandra replaced the phone on her cradle and fell back to the bed with a gentle bounce. *Yes.* Which question had her mother been answering with that one-word response? It didn't really matter, did it? A yes to any one of the questions pointed her in the same direction.

But Cassandra wasn't like her mother, or her elder sisters, where men were concerned. She didn't have their sense of adventure, their sense of confidence, their love of all things romantic. She was more cautious than the other female Kleins.

She was also the only one sleeping alone tonight.

Chapter 6

When Cassandra stopped her car at the Redmond Estate gates the next morning, three photographers started snapping away. She maintained her composure, and even turned her head toward the cameras for a moment to offer a professional and cool smile. She could not let them see that she was affected by their silly photographs and articles. She remained calm, even when one of the photographers winked and grinned in a suggestive way. Why did she get the feeling he was the one who'd snapped the picture of her bare legs?

Today the suit she wore was her most severe. The blouse was high-necked and the skirt hem fell well below her knee. The color was a limpid gray-green. Ms. Dunn adored this particular suit, and complimented Cassandra every time she wore it.

When the gates opened, she managed a small and

dismissive wave for the photographers—even the smarmy one.

Cassandra was greeted at the door by a flustered Oscar, and walked into a foyer that was crowded with suitcases and one very large trunk.

"What's going on?"

"They're leaving," Oscar said, obviously fretting. "I'm afraid I must've done something to offend them. Oh, it's all my fault. That one very large man, Jib…Jib…"

"Jibril," Cassandra said.

"Yes, I don't think he likes me. I offended him somehow, though I don't know what I might've done. They're angry because I helped the sheik escape for a while yesterday. I never should've done that." Oscar wrung wrinkled hands. "The sheik is the boss, I understand that, but if the others are angry with me, then he can't very well remain here. He's angry, too. Oh, he's in such a foul mood this morning, and it must be my fault. I failed at my job, and that's why they're all leaving."

"Don't be silly." Cassandra patted the old man's arm as she walked by. "I'm sure they're not going anywhere." The luggage said otherwise, but surely there was an explanation. "I have a tour of Silverton-upon-Kairn planned for today, and tomorrow…"

Kadir walked into the foyer, immediately claiming her full attention. Her heart fluttered…and she convinced herself it was because he had startled her with his brisk entrance.

"I'm afraid we won't be here tomorrow," he said crisply. Judging by the expression on his face, Oscar had been correct in his assessment of Kadir's mood. "As I have been informed that Lord Carrington is out of the country and will not return until shortly before the gala, there's no need for me to stay here."

Kadir walked toward one of the larger suitcases and Cassandra followed, her sensible heels clacking on the tile floor. "I'm sorry, Excellency. I had no idea Lord Carrington was leaving the country."

He turned and looked down at her, raising his eyebrows slightly at her formal use of the term Excellency. Still, others were listening. Well, Oscar was listening, and she had no desire to become the subject of estate staff gossip.

"There's no need to fly home," she said sensibly. "I have many activities planned for the coming two weeks. There's much more to Silvershire than a single meeting with Lord Carrington."

"I'm not going home," Kadir said. "My yacht is anchored in Leonia Bay, and I'm going to stay there for several days. I'm sorry to ruin your plans, but..." He glanced up, and Cassandra followed his gaze. Oscar had left the room, and they were truly alone—at least for the moment. "I'm not good at pretending, Cassandra," Kadir said in a lowered voice. "I don't believe I can see you each and every day and pretend that I don't want more than you're willing to give. This is for the best."

Since no one was watching, and there were no photographers nearby, she boldly looked him in the eye. "You're running away."

"Yes."

Cassandra shook her head in frustration. "Don't you understand that running will only make matters worse? People will assume that we either had a lover's spat, or that we're trying to pretend nothing happened."

His expression turned fierce. "I am trying to pretend that nothing happened!"

"Yes, but we can't *look* as if we're pretending."

"Cassandra..."

"Kadir."

When she said his name his expression softened. "You're testing me," he accused in a lowered voice.

"No, of course not." She was, however, very much testing herself. "Leonia is a lovely village. There are several nice restaurants in the area, and the view is lovely. It's a popular spot for a holiday."

"You've been there."

"My sister has a cottage just outside town. She's on vacation and has offered me the use of her home while she's away, so I have a place to stay while you live on your yacht. I'll continue to serve as your aide, of course, and we'll tour the area if you'd like. We can even go fishing. The photographers who are currently waiting outside the estate might follow, but within three days they will all be gone, because we won't give them anything interesting to photograph and nothing else ever happens in Leonia."

"Your plan is to bore them into leaving us alone."

"Precisely." It seemed like a logical enough plan, even worded so plainly.

Kadir looked her up and down, taking in the shoes, the conservative suit, the tightly restrained hair. "You will pack clothing more suitable for fishing than this dismal outfit?"

Dismal was a little harsh as a word choice to describe her suit, but... "Yes, of course."

Kadir studied her for a long moment, and she felt as if he were testing her somehow. He wanted distance from her. Distance would ruin her career. If he dumped her here while he went to his yacht for the duration of this visit, she'd be viewed as a failure. This was her most important assignment ever, and the man she'd been charged to assist couldn't run away from her.

"Go home and pack a bag," Kadir finally said. "We leave in one hour."

She almost did as he instructed, but a shimmer of warning stopped her. It looked as if the sheik and his entourage were ready to leave now. She couldn't take the chance that he'd leave her behind and she'd be forced to follow him to Leonia. She shouldn't be put in a position where she had to chase Kadir across the countryside.

"My sister and I wear the same size," Cassandra said. And there was a very nice little shop in town where she could buy those things she did not wish to borrow. Underwear, toothbrush, makeup—all the essentials. "I can leave whenever you're ready." She gave Kadir a professional smile.

Maybe he wanted to be rid of her, but she couldn't make herself easy to shake off. Besides, he'd soon realize that she was indispensable—as a political aide, of course.

Leonia Bay was indeed beautiful. Kadir had always loved being near the ocean, and he looked forward to settling in on his yacht.

But not right away, apparently. Cassandra offered a quick tour of the village, and he could not turn her down. Sayyid and Haroun accompanied them, while the others took a skiff weighted down with luggage to the yacht.

Only one of the photographers followed on the long trip from Silverton to Leonia, his older-model car keeping pace on the winding road. The others apparently thought they'd have a better chance of taking a marketable photo in the capital city. Cassandra was obviously concerned about the lone photographer. She didn't say so, of course, but her eyes flitted to the car often, and Kadir could see the worry in her eyes.

A woman like her should never have to worry. She should be pampered and protected and given all that she desired.

Haroun drove the conspicuous limousine through the picturesque town, and Sayyid kept a sharp eye on those they drove past. Tourists, retired couples, children…there was no obvious danger here. After making a quick stop at a small shop, they simply rode around for a while. Cassandra pointed out several interesting shops, a bakery that made wonderful cookies and fresh bread, the restaurants she preferred and a small museum that was very much unlike the Maitland Museum of Fine Arts in Silverton. This one was nautical in nature, and was not much bigger than the foyer of the Redmond Estate. Cassandra's dialogue was lively and professional and somewhat distant, considering that he still remembered what she'd tasted like just yesterday.

Kadir didn't understand Cassandra Klein, and he was a man who usually understood women quite well. She kissed like a woman who was interested in more than politics and propriety, and then she acted as if they had never kissed at all. She dressed conservatively, even gloomily, and yet now and then there was an intriguing gleam in her gray eyes that was anything but conservative or gloomy.

It had been a very long time since he'd met a woman who could take his mind entirely off his mission—and that was not a good thing. It would have been better if he'd left the Redmond Estate before her arrival this morning, as he had planned. Now that she was here, how was he going to get rid of her?

And he did need to get rid of her somehow. He could not possibly spend the next two weeks pretending that he didn't want her.

They ate lunch at a small, outdoor café that looked over the bay, drawing stares—since they were not dressed as the other tourists were, and Sayyid and Haroun were obviously bodyguards, not friends or guests. The photographer who had followed them from Silverton took a number of photographs, but the scene they presented was boring, as Cassandra had planned. To any eye, the lunch was purely professional.

The photographer soon turned his attention to different subjects—the sea, a pretty girl, three siblings who looked remarkably alike, but for their size. There was much beauty, many scenes of interest to an artist or a photographer in this small village. As the man with the camera wandered away from the café, Cassandra relaxed visibly.

She was very beautiful when she relaxed, and Kadir wished for his own camera to capture the expression on her face. Would he remember this moment clearly enough?

Cassandra was intent on keeping him busy throughout the day. Fishing was next on her list of things to do. She assured Kadir that her sister had all the proper equipment at her cottage. As they left the café she watched for the photographer to follow. He didn't. A pretty girl in a skimpy bathing suit had grabbed his attention, at least for the moment.

The cottage Cassandra spoke of was rather isolated,

located just beyond the edge of town and very near an outcropping of rocks that met the ocean waves. It was plain but neat, consisting of a main room, a kitchen, two bedrooms and two baths. All the rooms were large, which made the entire cottage feel airy and comfortable.

After checking the cottage thoroughly, Sayyid and Haroun positioned themselves at the entrances—Haroun on the front porch, Sayyid at the back door. Cassandra put on a pot of coffee, then disappeared into one of the bedrooms. After watching the closed door for a long moment, Kadir went to the wide window that looked out over the sea. The waves soothed him, as they often did, and he tried to take his mind off of Cassandra.

He knew how to be rid of her once and for all, but could he do it? Did he dare? It was not in his nature to be cruel, especially when he cared more than he should for the subject of that cruelty. And yet he had to do something. He had to take the matter in hand.

Cassandra exited the bedroom a few short minutes later, and he couldn't help but smile. She wore blue jeans that had been rolled up to just beneath her knees, tennis shoes with no socks and a pink T-shirt that advertised a local café—the very one where they'd eaten lunch. Her hair had been pulled back into a long, loose ponytail, and she looked years younger. She looked carefree and relaxed.

It was quite a transformation.

"I think these will fit you," she said, offering him a stack of clothes on outstretched arms. What she presented was worn blue jeans, much like hers, as well as a T-shirt. His was beige instead of pink. A pair of canvas shoes, stuffed with white socks, sat on top of the stack. He might've sent one of the bodyguards to the yacht to collect proper clothing for the afternoon's activities, but Cassandra had insisted it was not necessary. "They belong to Lexie's boyfriend, or one of her ex-husbands. I'm not sure which one, but they're more suitable for fishing than what you're wearing."

The suit he wore was dark and conservative and expensive, and definitely not intended for sea spray and live bait.

Cassandra glanced toward the front door. "Will your bodyguards want to fish with us? I can find old clothing for them, as well...."

"That won't be necessary," Kadir said as he headed for the bathroom so he could change his clothes. In order for his plan to get rid of Cassandra to work, he needed his bodyguards at a distance.

Cassandra hadn't been fishing in many years, but she still remembered how, for the most part. Kadir was very comfortable with a rod and reel, decked out in someone else's jeans and a snug-fitting T-shirt. When the wind caught his hair and blew it away from his face, and he looked so intent on his chore, he was quite fetching.

If a man could be fetching, that is, and if she could afford to notice. Which she couldn't.

Lexie's cottage was wonderfully secluded, so she didn't worry about curious eyes watching or listening. Well, other than Kadir's bodyguards, that is, and they weren't close enough to hear anything that was said. They remained alert, but the serenity of this place soothed even them, and she could almost forget that there were those who wanted Kadir dead, and these bodyguards were not a luxury but a necessity.

"Do you come here often?" Kadir asked, his eyes on the ocean.

"No."

"Why not?"

So, he wanted to add conversation to their fishing. It would be tricky, to be friendly with him without allowing things to proceed beyond friendly. "Lexie and I don't always get along. She and I are…very different." And that was putting it mildly.

"I have a villa on the ocean. Even in the worst of times, the water soothes me. I'm not sure why." Kadir sounded almost wistful, which surprised her. "I would rather be on my yacht than anywhere else in the world." He turned his head and looked at her, with those dark, bedroom eyes. "The living quarters are small, but very nice. You'd like them." For a long moment he was very thoughtful, and then he reeled in his line and turned to Sayyid. One step, and the bodyguard was all but rushing to meet him. The two men spoke in low tones, and it appeared that they were arguing with one another. And then, much to Cassandra's surprise, both bodyguards left.

Sayyid cast more than one glance back, but he and Haroun eventually got into the limo and drove back toward town.

"Where are they going?" Cassandra asked.

"Back to the yacht."

"But…"

"The photographer who followed us was left behind in town, snapping pictures of pretty girls and soothing scenery. No one knew in advance that I was coming here today. By tomorrow, word will be out, and anyone who knows the yacht is anchored here will arrive, and the possibility of danger will be real once again. But for today, just for today, no one knows where I am." His eyes on the ocean once again, he appeared to breathe deeper. He actually seemed to relax.

"How will you get back to the yacht?" Cassandra asked.

He shrugged his shoulders. "I'll call a taxi, or maybe I'll walk. A skiff will be left for me at the pier where we unloaded the luggage. That's no more than a mile from here, if I remember correctly. A pleasant enough walk."

They didn't catch anything at all, but the atmosphere was much more relaxed with the bodyguards gone. Kadir truly did look to be lost in the beauty of the ocean. In his position, did he have many truly free moments like this one? Probably not.

She wanted peaceful moments for Kadir, not because he was her first really big assignment, not because he was trying to change the state of his country for the better, not because his position was very much what she envisioned for herself, one day. She wanted him to have peaceful moments because she liked him. Not for the position he held, not for his dedication to making Kahani a better place. She liked *him.* His smile, his bedroom eyes, the way he kissed.

Time didn't stand still as they stood on the rocks and fished, but it did pass more slowly. Cassandra's heart rate slowed, and she breathed deeper than usual, taking in the sea air. The waves had a soothing rhythm that seemed to take on the cadence of her heart as she stood on the rocks and relaxed. It was very nice, and very *real,* and whether she would admit it or not, she liked simply being with Kadir, for a while.

But, of course, nothing good lasted forever. Eventually Kadir reeled in his line and walked toward her, fishing rod held casually in his hand. "We should head back to the yacht," he said. "It'll soon be time for dinner. You will join me, won't you?"

Cassandra reeled in her own line. "Dinner? Thanks for the invitation, but…" She'd planned on grabbing a can of soup from Lexie's cabinet. "I should get settled in here. You go ahead." He smiled at her, and suddenly eating a can of soup in Lexie's kitchen seemed very lonely.

"Sayyid left here with orders to have a catered supper waiting for the two of us. He was to go to one of the restaurants you pointed out today, the one you said was your favorite. You didn't mention which dish you preferred, so I asked that he have all of them made available."

Her heart skipped a beat. "All of them?"

They walked to the cottage, slowly and casually. This village, the cottage, the sea Kadir liked so much, they all had a way of doing that to a person—making them slow down and take deep breaths and relax. Cassandra almost never relaxed, but this was very nice. She hadn't known that she needed this holiday from her structured life, but apparently she did.

With the fishing gear stowed back in Lexie's storage shed, where they'd found it, Cassandra and Kadir began the walk toward the pier. For a few minutes, all was well. Kadir asked questions about Leonia and Lexie, and there was no talk of Lord Carrington or assassination attempts or alliances. Now and then he seemed to be about to say something, and then he changed his mind and turned the subject to something unimportant. The weather, fishing, food. All too soon she saw the pier ahead. A small skiff waited, as Kadir had said it would.

On the pier he turned to her, stopping so suddenly she almost ran into him. She stopped short, but not until she'd come so close she could smell the sea spray that had washed over him while they'd stood on the outcropping and fished the afternoon away. When she started to back away, he reached out one arm that encircled her and pulled her close. A strong hand settled at the small of her back, holding her firmly but gently in place.

"No eyes will be watching us tonight, Cassandra. Tomorrow that will change, but for tonight..."

"Don't," she said softly.

"I want you," Kadir said, ignoring her plea to stop before he went too far. "Sex between two adults who are obviously attracted to one another is nothing to be ashamed of. I know why you insist on hiding what you feel, but for tonight—just for tonight—why can't we take what we want? No one but the two of us ever needs to know."

A part of her was tempted, more tempted than she'd ever been or ever thought to be. She was drawn to Kadir, but was she willing to ruin her career for a flutter? Was any man worth throwing away years of planning and work and dedication?

As she was wondering, he leaned down and kissed her. No one was around to see, so she had no excuse to draw away. Besides, she wanted the kiss. She wanted the connection.

She wanted Kadir.

His mouth moved over hers, and she slipped her body closer to his. His arms held her close. She slipped her arms around his waist and held on as the kiss deepened. Her response was much more than a flutter, and she considered very seriously taking him up on his offer. There was more here than the desire for a sexual connection. She cared about this man she'd met less than a week ago. She cared very much.

It was Kadir who ended the kiss, taking his mouth from hers. "Say yes, and you won't be sorry," he whispered. "I won't allow you to be sorry."

The full weight of what she'd actually been considering hit her, and her knees wobbled. He meant something to her, in an unexpected way. But what did she mean to him? Did she mean anything at all? "I can't. You're asking me to throw away my job for a…a what? What is this, Kadir? A fling? A one-night stand? A diversion because you can't yet meet with Lord Carrington?"

"What does it matter?" he asked, more than slightly testy. "Do we have to give what's happening between us a name of some sort for you to file away in a neat box? Do all your relationships belong in a certain category, and until you know where I belong you're going to deny me, and yourself?"

She didn't want to tell him that *all her relationships* were…him.

"I'm not asking you to run away with me," he said sharply. "I'm just asking for one night. Just because we're working together, that doesn't mean we can't also enjoy a casual sexual relationship. It's been a difficult week. Sex will help us to relax."

It was easy to step away after he said that. She was drawn to him; he liked her. But she wasn't about to endanger her career for *one night.* She wasn't about to throw it all away for *casual.* "I think you should have dinner alone," she said sharply as she backed away from him.

"And tomorrow?" he asked, his voice remaining sharp. "Will you once again don a drab suit that does not suit you and pretend that nothing happened?"

"Nothing did happen," she insisted.

"Pity," Kadir said. He jumped into the waiting skiff and quickly untied the lines that lashed it to the dock. Before starting the engine, he turned those dark eyes to her. "Call the Ministry of Foreign Affairs and tell them I require another aide for the duration of my visit. One who is more…hospitable." He glanced to the west, where the sun had already disappeared behind the horizon. "It's almost dark. Wait here. I'll send Sayyid back with the keys to the limousine. He will drive you home."

Speechless, Cassandra watched him steer the skiff toward the waiting yacht. For a few moments she didn't move at all. His last words had been cruel, and she had not thought him capable of cruelty. Had he only been charming when he'd thought she'd sleep with him? The kissing, the fishing, the smiles… Had they been a part of his attempted seduction?

And what would Ms. Dunn say when she called and requested that someone else be assigned to His Excellency during the remainder of his time in Silvershire?

The skiff disappeared as it rounded the yacht. Maybe there was a ladder or something on the other side of the large vessel. He'd tie up the skiff, climb the ladder—anger took the place of her confusion and hurt, and Cassandra's attitude took a sharp turn—and choke on his romantic dinner for two.

As she allowed anger—which was much easier for her to manage than the initial hurt—to take over, she realized that she was much better off discovering this crude side of Kadir's nature now, rather than later. His charm had disguised the seedier side of his nature, and he'd almost had her fooled. Almost. She'd been so close to making a mistake she'd have regretted for the rest of her life.

No way was she going to stand here and wait for Sayyid or anyone else to collect her and drive her back to Lexie's cottage. She was perfectly capable of walking there, even if she ended up arriving after the night turned pitch black. Cassandra left the pier and stalked to the road that would lead her back to the cottage, glad for the opportunity to walk off some of her anger.

How dare he? It had all been a game to him, one seduction in a line of many, and she'd almost taken him seriously. Tears threatened, but she pushed them away. Al-Nuri didn't deserve her tears. He was a macho, spoiled, demanding *pig.* If there was ever a time for her to be the ice maiden Lexie had called her in the past…

She hadn't taken two steps down the road before a thundering explosion startled her breathless, and she spun toward the ocean as a fireball claimed Kadir's yacht. Another explosion followed, sending flames into the air and ragged pieces of the once fine vessel into the sea.

She was stunned for a moment, and then the truth hit her between the eyes like a sharp-bladed knife. Kadir was on that yacht.

Unable to control her own legs, Cassandra dropped to her knees and started to scream.

Chapter 7

Cassandra didn't have her cell phone with her, but as it turned out she didn't need one. By the time she stopped screaming, she heard the approaching sirens. Of course, everyone in town had seen the explosion. Local authorities would take charge, they would search for survivors in the sea and begin an investigation.

She'd seen the explosion, and she didn't think there would be any survivors for the authorities to find. Bodies, yes, but survivors…no.

She gave a brief and almost hysterical statement to the officer who assisted her from the road. Leonia had a local police force, but it was small and the officers were unaccustomed to dealing with anything of this magnitude. As she watched the authorities scramble to handle the situation, she had one clear thought. A call to Ms. Dunn would get proper investigators on the scene quickly. Whoever had done this must be made to pay.

But no amount of justice would bring Kadir, or the other people who'd been on that yacht, back. It was so unfair, so *wrong.*

The same officer who took her statement, such as it was, drove Cassandra back to the cottage. He asked her if she needed help, if she needed a doctor or someone to sit with her for a while, but she declined. She wanted to be alone. She wanted to cry some more and scream again, and she couldn't do that with this stranger, or any other, watching her.

Inside the cottage, Cassandra called Ms. Dunn and passed on the news about the explosion and Kadir's death in an insanely calm voice. Tears stung her eyes, but she didn't allow her boss to hear those tears in her voice. Still, apparently the astute Ms. Dunn heard *something.*

"Cassie, are you all right?" the older woman asked when the short report was completed.

"I'm…" The word *fine* stuck in her throat. She could've been on that yacht when it had exploded, but she hadn't been. She was safe because she'd allowed Kadir's less-than-romantic invitation to sway her decision, because she was the ice maiden Lexie accused her of being, because when love had presented itself to her, it hadn't come in the neat, pretty package she'd expected, so she'd thrown it away. Her knees wobbled, and she was forced to sit on the floor, phone still in hand.

"I prefer to be called Cassandra," she said in a too-soft voice.

"Of course," Ms. Dunn replied gently.

Her anger flared, pushing away the confusion. "Sheik Kadir was a very nice man, you know. Smart, funny, dedicated to his country the way we are dedicated to ours. He didn't deserve to die this way. Whoever Lord Carrington sends to investigate the explosion—the *assassination*—make sure they're the best. I want those responsible caught and I want them to be punished."

"Of course. I would have it no other way, Cassandra." There was a short, expectant pause before the woman added, "I'm going to send Timothy Little to Leonia tomorrow to collect you." Once again, Ms. Dunn's voice was all business, if not quite as sharp as usual.

Cassandra had no desire to see the overly eager diplomatic aide Ms. Dunn offered to send, or anyone else from the office. She wanted—needed—to be alone. "No, thank you. I'm going to stay here for a few days." There was no way she could return home now, and she certainly couldn't go back to the ministry tomorrow or the next day as if nothing had happened. Her brain wasn't working correctly, and her heart was broken in so many ways she didn't know how it could ever be fixed. How could any man do this to her in just a few days? How could Kadir matter to her so much that his death and the knowledge that she would never see him again devastated her, when in truth she barely knew him?

"Yes, certainly, if that's what you want, Cassandra," Ms. Dunn agreed. "Call me when you get the chance. I'd like to know that you're doing well."

"Of course."

When the call was done, Cassandra remained on the floor. Her legs were weak still, so she leaned against the couch and hugged herself with trembling arms. She did her best to ignore the tears that dripped down her cheeks. She needed to call her mother before the news of Kadir's death began to spread, but...not now. Not yet. She needed to be better composed before she spoke to her mum. For now, she was content to sit on the floor and allow the emotions she'd tried to deny wash over her.

Instead of throwing herself wholeheartedly into what she'd felt for Kadir from the moment she'd seen him, she'd allowed her reservations to keep her at a distance. Even when he'd kissed her, when she'd kissed him, her misgivings had come between them and she'd held so much of herself back. Why couldn't she be more like Lexie? More bold where men were concerned. More daring. Why did she find it impossible to take even the smallest chance?

If she'd invited Kadir to come into the cottage to share a can of soup, he'd still be alive. He might've stayed and kissed her some more. Perhaps on this very couch. He would've held her closely, if she'd allowed it. Would she have? She didn't know, and she'd never have the chance to find out. If she hadn't been so damned concerned about her career, she would have a warm memory or two of the man who caused her stomach to flutter.

If she'd given in to her feelings, she wouldn't feel as if she'd thrown away the only man she'd ever loved.

If, if, if. Cassandra lay down on the floor and covered her face with her hands, as if she could hide in that childish way. Shaking, dry-eyed, terrified—she could not imagine that she'd ever have the energy or the drive to get up off the floor.

This was what she'd been trying to avoid in being cautious, and look where it had gotten her. She'd kept Kadir at a distance, she'd maintained her professional attitude—for the most part. She'd done her best to keep him and his flutters at a distance…and still her heart was broken.

* * *

Amala ran on the beach, laughing and skipping, as little girls did. Kadir tried to catch her, but he couldn't quite keep up. His big sister was older than him by three years, and even hampered by a skirt that brushed the sand, she ran faster than he did. Her legs were much longer and even stronger than his own, and she pulled away from him, slowly and then with a speed that stole his breath away.

Suddenly Kadir knew something bad was about to happen. Dark clouds moved in, and the waves grew tall and threatening. Amala pulled farther away from him. He tried to run faster, but instead it seemed his legs wouldn't move at all.

A wave washed over the sand, grabbed a screaming Amala…and then she vanished, lost to the sea.

When Amala was gone, the wave came for Kadir. He stood there, unable to move or to say a word, while it rose up above him, broke down and swallowed him like a monster made of saltwater. The water was in his eyes, in his mouth, and it tried to drag him down.

He reached out in desperation, but the monster was too much for a small boy to fight and he could no longer breathe….

With a gasp, Kadir reached out. His hand found a ledge of sharp rock. Another wave—just a wave, not a monster—tried to grab him, but he held on tightly to the rock. He blinked the stinging, salty water out of his eyes, and gasped for air. He hurt everywhere. He could barely breathe. And if he wasn't careful, the next wave might pull him down and down, and there would be no coming back up.

The sky was dark, with nothing but a half-moon to

light the waves and the jagged rock. There was a moment, not much more than a second or two, when Kadir believed he was trapped in a dream. But then he remembered.

He'd been about to climb the ladder that would take him on board his yacht when his conscience had forced him to change his mind. True, his treatment of Cassandra would send her away, as planned…but faced with the reality of his success, he didn't want her to believe that he didn't care for her at all. He didn't want her to think he was a shallow playboy who cared only for women who would come to his bed when called.

So he'd turned the skiff around and headed for the pier. He'd watched, in the dying light of day, as Cassandra stalked away from the pier, not waiting for Sayyid as he had instructed her to do. She was angry, rightfully so. All he had to do for his heartless plan to succeed was allow her to continue to be angry….

And then the first explosion had come without warning. Kadir had been blown into the water. The blast stole his breath, and tossed him from the boat as if he weighed nothing. Before he fell into the waves, something—a sharp piece of flying debris—cut into his arm. The skiff was tossed and broken, and he sank. The other explosion had come as he'd been fighting to find the surface, and then…darkness.

He wasn't sure how he'd survived. Somehow he'd fought his way to the surface for air, but he didn't remember doing so. Somehow he'd floated or swum or drifted to this piece of rocky shore—but he had no recollection of making his way here. Perhaps those memories would return to him in time, but then again, they might not.

He had the fleeting and nonsensical feeling that his sister, Amala, who'd been dead for fifteen years, had somehow guided him to the surface. For a moment he was quite sure that the spirit of his sister had saved him from the monster of the sea.

It was with great effort that Kadir pulled himself onto the rock, using his left arm for leverage since his right was unusually weak. He lay back, exhausted and unable to move, while his mind began to clear somewhat.

After a few moments, he asked himself the question. Who was responsible for the explosion? Who had known he would be on the yacht tonight? Who would've been able to get word to Zahid that tonight was the proper time and place for assassination? His bodyguards. Hakim and Tarif. The lone photographer, whose name he did not know. The small and trusted staff on the yacht.

And Cassandra.

He didn't want to believe she could be involved, but she had refused his invitation to join him for the evening—not that he had bothered to make the invitation suitable for a woman like her—and that refusal had kept her safe from the blast.

In truth, anyone might be behind the explosion. Zahid's followers had kidnapped Mukhtar's family in order to force the old man to do as they wished. They were not above doing the same again, which meant he could trust no one.

No one.

Without the sun to warm the rock and his body, the night very quickly turned cool. A breeze on his wet clothing made Kadir shudder. His life had not been entirely safe for the past fifteen years, but he had always had people around him he could trust completely. Zahid had not always been an immediate threat, and there had been moments of peace, and people he could rely upon without fail.

But somehow, amidst his determination to bring about change and stop Zahid and his followers, Kadir had managed to separate himself from almost everyone, even those who had earned his trust. He was no longer close to his brothers; in truth, he barely knew them anymore. Their wives and children were strangers. Women came and went, none ever getting too close to his heart. For fifteen years he had kept a shield between him and everyone else in his life.

Why did it seem, at this moment, that he was more alone than he had ever been? Why did it seem that he could trust no one but the dead? His parents. Amala. Everyone who had been on the yacht when it exploded.

He grew so cold he was compelled to move off the rock and toward the road, though he had no destination in mind. Where does a man go when he can truly trust no one? He walked slowly, up the jagged rock and across a collection of loose pebbles, before finding himself on the narrow road. And there, directly before him, was Cassandra's cottage.

Her sister's cottage, to be more precise. Illumination from inside warmed one window with yellowish light. Other windows were dark. Was she there, sitting in that one lighted room? Or was she in the darkened room, not alone but with a man? A lover. Zahid, perhaps. Had she been putting on an act for him all this time? Was Cassandra Klein one of Zahid Bin-Asfour's converts? Maybe she was simply his mistress….

Light-headed and more confused than he had ever

been, Kadir closed his eyes tightly. No, he could trust Cassandra. She had nothing to gain by aligning herself with Zahid. And...she would not. She was a modern woman, a woman who valued her career and her independence. Cassandra was everything Zahid despised.

Cassandra was everything Amala would've liked to have been, but Amala had not been given the same opportunities. If she had, would she be alive today?

Kadir walked toward the lighted window. He must be cautious; he must always be cautious. But when the day arrived when he could truly trust no one in the world...he would just as soon be dead.

Sleep was impossible. Maybe she would never sleep again.

Cassandra sat on Lexie's small couch, a light blanket wrapped around her shoulders to ward off the chill that had nothing to do with the temperature of the air. Two lamps burned in this main room. The rest of the cottage was dark.

She'd telephoned her parents, before it got too late, to assure them that she was fine. If she didn't call and they heard she was here, they'd jump in the car and drive overnight and be here by morning. She wasn't ready for company—not even theirs—so she'd told them Ms. Dunn had offered to send someone to collect her and drive her back to Silverton. She didn't bother to note that she'd declined the offer.

A soft knock at the back door caught her so by surprise, she twitched sharply. At this time of night it could only be bad news. Maybe Lexie had returned because she and Stanley had had a fight and the vacation was over. Maybe the police had found Kadir's body.

That thought caused a bone-deep shiver. Maybe Ms. Dunn had ignored Cassandra's insistence that she was going to stay here for a few days, and Tim Little was here to collect her.

But why hadn't she heard a car?

Cassandra stood and dropped the blanket from her shoulders. Once again, the soft knock—a scraping, almost—came from the direction of the back door.

Someone had killed Kadir. Did that same someone want her dead, too? Lexie kept a small, old revolver in the drawer of her desk. They had argued over that weapon on Cassandra's last visit. Lexie said she needed some sort of protection in the remote house, even though nothing much ever happened in Leonia. Cassandra had argued that Lexie was more likely to accidentally shoot herself with that six-shooter.

But now Cassandra rushed to the desk, opened the drawer and withdrew the weapon. She didn't know much about guns. Was it even loaded? Was the safety on? She looked for a safety as she walked into the kitchen, but didn't see one anywhere on the gun. Maybe all she had to do was point and shoot.

That was the big question. Could she point this weapon at a human being and shoot to kill? The uncertainty didn't last long. If the person who'd killed Kadir was on the other end of the gun, she'd have no trouble pulling the trigger.

Again, the knock—which was not quite a knock, but was once again more of a scraping—sounded. Maybe what she heard on the other side of the door was an animal. If it was any of the people she'd first thought of, she would've heard a car. If it was a person planning to do her harm, they likely wouldn't knock at all. It would be easy enough for an intruder to break the glass, reach inside and unlock the door. Yes, maybe what she heard was an animal who'd wandered onto the back porch.

She kept the six-shooter in her hand, just in case.

At the back door, Cassandra stood to one side and lifted the curtain that covered the four small windowpanes. Even though the light in the kitchen was off, she saw nothing beyond the window but darkness. Maybe it had been an animal, after all—a wandering dog, perhaps—and the creature had already moved on. She'd almost relaxed when a hand shot out of the darkness and pressed against a pane of glass she'd unveiled. Her heart jumped, she raised the gun and then a soft voice said, "Cassandra?"

She knew that voice. Hands trembling, she unlocked the door and opened it wide. Kadir stood there, leaning beside the door as if that was the only way he could continue to stand. He was wet, his eyes were strangely unfocused and his clothes were torn and bloody.

But he wasn't dead.

She reached out and took his wrist in her hand, drawing him gently into the kitchen.

Once he was inside the kitchen, she closed the door and placed the six-shooter on the counter. When she reached for the light switch, Kadir stopped her with a whispered, "Don't. Someone might be watching." Those words of caution reminded her to lock the door again, before leading Kadir into the main room and the light of two lamps, so she could study him more closely. Here the windows were tightly covered, so they didn't need to worry about prying eyes.

She supported him with an arm around his waist, as he walked slowly toward the couch where moments earlier she'd been grieving for him. His right arm was bleeding, she noted, and he shivered to the bone.

When they reached the couch, he all but fell onto it. Cassandra put her panic aside and assessed what had to be done immediately, then she reached for the phone.

Kadir moved quickly, much more quickly than she'd thought him capable of, and clamped his hand tightly around her wrist. "Don't call anyone."

Obviously he wasn't thinking clearly. He'd had quite a shock, and might be delirious. "You need a doctor. When that's taken care of I'll call Ms. Dunn, and she'll contact the proper authorities in Kahani. Would you prefer to make that call yourself? Someone needs to get started with those calls right away. Everyone thinks you're dead, Kadir. We need to let them know—"

"No," he said sharply. "No doctor. No phone calls." His eyes met hers, and she saw in his gaze that while he was still not himself, he was thinking clearly. He was not delusional. "If everyone thinks I'm dead, this is a good thing. For now, at least. I don't know who I can trust, Cassandra. Only you. Tonight I trust only you."

She returned the phone to its place on the end table and covered Kadir with the blanket. "Your arm is bleeding."

"Is it?" He glanced at the torn and bloody sleeve and the damaged flesh beneath as if he had not yet realized he was wounded. "So it is. You'll have to bandage it for me."

"I'm not a doctor."

"No, but your medical care will suffice. It has to, for now. If word gets out that I'm alive, we will both be in danger." He reached out his left hand to caress her face. "I have always known that my life could be cut short by those who oppose me. But you—you should not be put in harm's way because you're with me. If you cannot keep my secret, if you must call someone and tell them I'm alive, then I'll leave right now. By staying with you I could bring those who would kill a dozen people or more in order to get to me, those who murdered everyone on that yacht because they thought I was there, to your door. I won't do that."

Cassandra leaned down and gave Kadir a quick kiss. She touched him, her fingers brushing against his damp shirt and then his too-cool hand. Her mind and her heart were still reeling with the knowledge that he was alive. That he was here. That he trusted her.

"I won't call anyone." She'd doctor him as best she could, telling him again and again that she was relieved beyond belief to see him alive. She wanted to kiss him again, once his arm was bandaged and she dressed him in warm, dry clothes. And after that?

Cassandra had no idea where they were headed or what would happen next. She did know that they had no choice but to deal with "after that" tomorrow.

Chapter 8

Kadir woke with a start, gasping as if reaching desperately for air.

Unlike the last time he came to consciousness with such ferocity, he found himself warm and dry, lying in a soft bed, safe and secure—and not alone. He assessed the situation quickly. His arm had been cleaned and bandaged. He remembered Cassandra leaning over him and tending the wound with great care. She slept beside him now, her warm curves close to his body. Her slumber was deep, but one of her small feet was draped over one of his legs, as if she had arranged herself to awaken if he dared to leave the bed or even roll away from her.

Morning was coming, after a night so long he could not fathom that twenty-four hours ago he had been sleeping at the Redmond Estate. A touch of light turned the sky beyond the bedroom window gray, as a new day approached.

But morning had not yet arrived, and for the first time in a very long time Kadir relaxed completely. There were no bodyguards at the ready, no precautions to be taken, no danger waiting outside the bedroom door. Everyone but Cassandra thought he'd been on the yacht when it exploded. Zahid and whoever had betrayed Kadir thought he was dead.

At the moment Kadir liked being dead. He liked it very much. As he reached for Cassandra, wanting only to stroke his fingers against her warm skin, sleep crept upon him, gently and completely.

The jangling of the phone woke Cassandra, and she came awake with a start. The ringing woke Kadir, too. He sat up and looked at her, not yet fully alert. Cassandra took a deep breath and reached for the bedside phone, answering with a sleepy "Hello."

Cassandra relaxed as her greeting was returned. It was Ms. Dunn calling, asking if she'd changed her mind about being collected by Timothy Little and being brought back to Silverton. There was work to be done at the Ministry of Foreign Affairs, Ms. Dunn imparted sharply. Particularly so at this time as the Founder's Day Galà was just two weeks away. Two weeks from yesterday, to be precise.

Ms. Dunn was of the opinion that hard work was the proper cure for any ailment—including the shock of watching a yacht filled with innocents being blown out of the water.

It was the older woman's way of checking in with Cassandra and assuring herself that all was well in the cottage in Leonia. She would never come right out and ask, but

Cassandra had worked with Ms. Dunn long enough to know what the intentions of the call really were.

Cassandra assured her boss that she still wanted to take a few days off, and that she'd return to Silverton by the end of the week. She didn't know if that was true or not—she had no idea when she'd return to Silverton—but it would do for now.

With Ms. Dunn properly and completely dismissed, Cassandra turned her attention to Kadir. "How do you feel this morning?"

"Better," he said. "Much better."

He looked much better. In fact, he looked large and handsome and healthy and well-rested. There was some stubble around his usually well-trimmed beard and mustache, and his black hair was mussed. She imagined this was what he always looked like in the morning—stubbly and warm, with his longish hair slightly wild and very curly, and his eyes, his bedroom eyes, dark and sleepy and filled with a promise she did not entirely understand.

Last night she had helped him dress in a pair of cotton pajama bottoms that likely belonged to Stanley. They had not seen much wear, and fit well enough. But his chest was bare, and it was the finely sculpted, slightly hairy chest of a real man. She should move away…but she didn't.

"How's the arm?" Her eyes dropped to the bandage on his right biceps, and Kadir's gaze traveled there, as well.

"Fine. You're a good doctor." He actually managed a small smile, one she returned.

She tried to sound as if she were completely unaffected to be sharing a bed with this man. "The cut wasn't as bad as it looked at first, but we'll have to keep an eye on it and make sure it doesn't get infected."

Now that they were awake, she really should scramble out of the bed and put some distance between her and the man she'd slept with last night. It wasn't entirely necessary that she be here. She could've retired to the other bedroom last night—but Kadir had still been mostly out of it when she'd put him to bed, and she'd been half-afraid that if she left him here alone, in the morning he'd be gone as if his appearance at the kitchen door last night had been nothing more than a dream, or the magical answer to a heartfelt wish.

But this morning he remained very real.

Kadir scooted closer to her, and she did not back away from the blatant advance. He wrapped one arm around her, and she took a deep breath that filled her lungs with his scent as she swayed very slightly in his direction. One of her hands settled against his bare midsection. Yes, he was warmer than he had been last night, fresh out of the sea and stunned by the explosion. He felt more solid, more real, more *safe.* Her hand remained there, pressed lightly to his muscled abdomen. It was a nice, comforting reminder that he was real and alive and *here.*

"I thought you were dead," she whispered. "I saw the yacht explode, and in my mind you were already on it and…" The rest caught in her throat. "What happened? Were you thrown clear?" She didn't see how that was possible, but Kadir was here, so obviously something had happened.

"I wasn't on the yacht when it exploded," he said, his mouth settling near her throat, there where shoulder curved into neck. A quiet quiver passed through her body in response to that contact. "I had a change of heart and was returning to you."

In order to try again to seduce her? In order to tell her again that she was not suitable as an aide? At the moment, she didn't care what had made him turn around and come back to her. Turning back had saved his life, and she could only be glad.

"I didn't want you to think that I didn't care about you," he said softly. "Even though I knew it was best if you remained angry with me, even though I purposely pushed you away, I didn't want to leave things between us unpleasant. I do care for you, Cassandra."

Was he saying that because they were in bed together, dressed in nothing more than skimpy nightclothes that could be easily discarded? Or was he sincere? At this moment she didn't care why he said he cared for her. The words sounded true to her jaded ears, and so she accepted what he said. It was enough, for now.

In trying so hard to be independent and carefree of heart, she'd thrown away a chance at knowing true passion. She wouldn't throw it away again.

She shifted her head and nuzzled Kadir. She tasted his neck, his jaw, and finally brought his mouth to hers and kissed him deeply. Her entire body shuddered, and she instinctively pressed herself more securely against him. This time there was nothing and no one to stop her. No second thoughts, no worry about her heart. It was impossible to guard the heart completely without shutting it down. Turning it off and denying moments like this, in order to remain free of heartbreak, also robbed her of a chance at knowing passion.

She didn't care if Kadir broke her heart, eventually. All she cared about was now. This moment, this touch, this celebration of the fact that he was alive.

And so was she.

The kiss was not desperate, but it was far from sweet. A depth she had never suspected was possible arose and grew in the meeting of two mouths. The kiss fused Kadir to her in a way that went beyond the physical, beyond the mere meeting of lips and teasing of tongues.

Kadir's hand held her head, fingers speared through her hair. His beard was rough, and at times she felt it scraping across her chin or her cheek, but she didn't care. Their lips barely touched, and then fused together. The kiss was light for a moment, and then it deepened. Her heart beat hard, her blood raced, and as for the flutter…it grew swiftly to something well beyond a mere flutter. She had never wanted anything so much….

"Cassandra," Kadir whispered, pulling his mouth from hers for only a moment.

If he asked her if she was sure about what was about to happen, she might falter, so she didn't allow him to say more. She spread her fingers through his curls and pulled his mouth to hers, tight and firm. She slipped her tongue deep into his mouth and wrapped one leg over his hip. He was right there, with nothing but a few scraps of fabric between them. Was she sure? *Yes,* more sure than she had ever been.

He slipped his fingers just barely into the waistband of the pajamas she'd borrowed from Lexie's chest of drawers. Fingers brushed against skin no man had ever touched before, and she quivered. She quivered intensely, and a sound crept up her throat and escaped as something near a moan. It was a sound she had never made before.

Kadir's hand slipped lower, and she found herself arching slightly to bring him closer. Closer and closer…

When the phone rang, she jumped, but she did not roll over. She kissed Kadir more deeply, then drew her well-kissed lips away and whispered against his mouth, "They'll call back."

He made a sound much like her little moan, and answered, "Or else they will come here to the cottage to check on you. We don't want that." The phone had rung three times. Four. Five. Another kiss. Six. With a groan, Cassandra rolled over and snatched at the receiver.

"Hello!"

She scooted slightly farther away from Kadir. "Oh, hi, Mum."

"Is everything all right?" The voice on the phone held all the concern of a woman for her daughter. More than anyone, Piper Klein understood how much Cassandra had come to care for Kadir. What timing. Almost-psychic Mum strikes again.

"Yes. I…you woke me up." Cassandra sat up, not quite at ease to remain entangled with Kadir while she spoke to her mother.

"I'm sorry. You're usually up so early, I just assumed you'd be awake by now. I know you had a late night, and…oh, honey, I'm so sorry. We can come up there to stay with you for a few days, or we can meet you in Silverton."

She'd made the same offer last night, and Cassandra had declined. She did so again. "No, thank you. That's not necessary. Ms. Dunn is urging me to get back to work as soon as possible. I think she believes staying busy will help. I might head back this afternoon and take her advice." She hated lying to her mother, but what choice did she have? "I'm fine, Mum, truly I am."

The bed creaked and undulated as Kadir rolled away and off the other side. He headed for the bathroom, closing the door behind him.

Cassandra turned her back on the bathroom door.

She wanted, so much, to tell her mother that Kadir was alive. But she couldn't do that. Not only would it mean breaking her word to Kadir, it could very well put Piper Klein into a dangerous situation. In a lowered voice she said, "You were right when you said I've been too cautious. I should've thrown myself at Sheik Kadir the moment he walked off the plane and those flips and flutters appeared and surprised me. I should've told him the first night that I knew when I first saw him that he was the one for me."

"You've always been prudent."

"I've always been afraid," Cassandra replied. She heard the shower begin to run. She could speak more loudly now, since Kadir was occupied and the shower would mask her words even more than the closed door, but she didn't. Her voice remained soft. "I've always been afraid of being hurt the way Lexie has been, so many times. She was always so desperately heart-broken when an affair or a marriage ended, and seeing her that way scared me. I only want what you and Daddy have."

"One day you'll have it." The promise sounded less than authentic, like a mother telling a small child that one day her Prince Charming will arrive on a white horse and after that there would be happily ever after.

"Maybe," Cassandra answered. "But I won't get it by being afraid all the time and not even allowing myself to try. I suppose I could take a few lessons from Lexie."

"Let's not take this to extremes!"

Cassandra laughed lightly at her mother's hint of panic. "I'm still me, Mum. I'm just..." Different. Bolder. Less afraid. "God, I feel like I'm a hundred years older than I was this time yesterday."

Piper Klein sighed into the phone. "That's it. I'm coming to Leonia today."

"Don't do that. I might not even be here this afternoon. I really might decide to take Ms. Dunn up on her offer of burying myself in work." She told her mother again that she was fine, and then she hung up the phone and fell back onto the bed, wishing Kadir was still here with her.

The shower continued to run on the other side of the bathroom door. Kadir was in there, naked. She knew he wanted her. He had always wanted her. She'd been the one who'd put on the brakes, time and time again. She'd been the one to insist that their relationship remain professional.

She walked toward the bathroom door, unbuttoning the pajama top as she went. These pajamas had been a Christmas gift from Mum, but apparently they were too conservative for Lexie, because until last night they'd never been worn. They still had that crisp fold of newness, and until last night the tag had still been on the pants. No, Lexie slept in sexy lingerie—or nothing at all. She knew how to seduce a man. Cassandra did not. Her mouth was dry with nervousness, and she was a woman who never allowed herself a moment of nervousness.

She opened the bathroom door without knocking. Kadir's slightly distorted figure beyond the steamy shower glass was intriguing and arousing. He was tall and lean, but not too lean. He had nicely honed muscles and a pleasantly masculine shape, and what she'd felt in the bed had only been a hint of the possibilities that lay ahead. She allowed the unbuttoned pajama top to slip off and hit the floor.

Before she could take a step toward the shower and the naked man within it, a deep voice stopped her with a single word.

"Don't."

Puzzled, she stood in the middle of the bathroom, half-dressed. "Don't what?"

"Don't step into this shower with me," Kadir said. His voice was just loud enough for her to be sure she heard every word clearly. "Don't have sex with me simply because you're relieved I'm not dead."

"Kadir, I'm not…"

"And don't lie. Not to me and not to yourself. It's easy to get caught up in what I want when you're kissing me, when your body is warm against mine, but stepping away gave me time to think. You have resisted me until now. What's changed?"

She recognized that whatever might've happened if her mother hadn't called likely wasn't going to happen now. "Maybe you think too much," she argued.

What might've been a rough, humorless laugh that didn't last long rumbled from the shower. "I wish I didn't have to think at all, but I have no choice. There is one man in the world I can trust, and I've not yet decided how I might get in touch with him without alerting others to my survival." In a lower voice he added, "There is one woman in the world I can trust. If I sleep with her in her moment of weakness, if I take advantage of her obvious relief that I find myself still among the living, will she come to regret what should never be cause for regret?"

"I won't…"

"You don't know, not today. Not this morning, when it seems there's no one else in the world but the two of us." She heard his remorse, and it made her sad. "We're not alone in the world, Cassandra, and before much longer it's going to come crashing in on us with a vengeance. When that happens, will you still feel as you do now?"

"I could promise you I won't have regrets, but you're not going to believe me, are you?"

"Not today," he said softly.

"All right." Cassandra picked up the pajama top from the floor and carried it into the bedroom, closing the bathroom door behind her. She didn't cry. Tears were for death and destruction and heartbreak, not simple failures. That's what this was, after all. A failure. She was a failure at seduction.

She slipped on the pajama top and buttoned it as she left the bedroom. A large breakfast was called for, and she didn't remember what Lexie had in her kitchen. Surely the makings for pancakes or muffins were in the cupboard.

No, she didn't cry, and she didn't get a little angry. Her mind whirled with possibilities and plans and scenarios. Maybe she was a failure as a seductress, but she hadn't had any practice in the past so she had to start from scratch. Since she had no doubts that Kadir wanted her, she didn't think the task would be too terribly difficult.

And even though she had failed, thus far, she wasn't about to give up. What she'd wanted had changed, but her personality had not. She was still a sledgehammer, and she still went after everything she wanted with fierce determination.

A heavenly scent assaulted Kadir as he left the bedroom behind. Sweet and cinnamony, the smells of something baking filled the house. He'd been afraid that Cassandra would take offense at his refusal of her proposition, but that was a chance he had to take. A woman didn't change her mind overnight. Well, sometimes she did, but it was never a well-thought-out change of intentions. It was nice that she was relieved to find him alive, but he didn't want Cassandra to sleep with him this morning, and lament doing so by the time night fell once again.

But since he heard cheerful humming drifting from the kitchen, along with the heavenly smell, she had apparently survived his refusal quite well.

She still wore her pajamas, he saw as he stepped into the kitchen. He himself had found some clothes in the spare bedroom closet, which came very close to fitting him, as the fishing clothes had done yesterday. Worn blue jeans, a green cotton button-up shirt and worn deck shoes would do until he could buy something new.

With what, he did not know. He was wealthy man, but he had no cash on him and he was believed to be dead.

"Do you like muffins?" Cassandra asked as she peeked into the oven. "Hmmm. Almost done. Another three or four minutes, I'd guess." She stood and turned, and when she saw his face her smile faded and he actually saw her twitch. "Good heavens, what have you done?"

Kadir laid a hand on his smooth cheek. "I shaved." He did not tell her that the idea of shaving had originally come from glimpsing the redness of her cheeks and chin after they'd kissed. He did not want to hurt her, not even in that small way. "I would like those who believe me to be dead to continue in that belief. After we eat those muffins, I would like for you to cut my hair. With the physical changes and other certain precautions, no one will recognize me."

Once her shock faded, she smiled in obvious approval. "I like it. You look younger without the beard, and—" she cocked her head slightly and studied him well "—different. The clothes make a big difference, too. Once we cut your hair, only someone who knows you very well will recognize you."

He didn't bother to tell Cassandra that it was likely someone who knew him very well who had been the one to betray him.

She walked toward him, still seeming not at all disturbed by what he had counted on as being a bone of contention. Most women did not take rejection so well. Maybe she'd recognized that he was right in calling an end to what had almost happened in her bed. That was always possible. Not likely, but possible. Cassandra Klein was a sensible woman, after all.

Upon reaching him, she lifted her hand and touched his cheek. "Nice." And then she went up on her toes and laid her mouth over his.

She kissed him. Her arms did not go around him; his did not go around her. Still, his body responded. His very world tilted.

And then she dropped away, with a smile on her face. "No need to look at me that way, Kadir. I had to know what it was like to kiss you without the beard, now didn't I?"

It sounded like a woman's convoluted reasoning, but he didn't dare to argue with her.

As if nothing had happened, she said, "The muffins are ready. I hope you're hungry. A woman can't just make two or three muffins, so we might as well eat hearty."

If the kiss was Cassandra's idea of revenge, if it was her way of tossing his well-meant refusal back in his face and making him taste regret all over again—then she was winning this particular battle.

So Kadir did the only thing he could think of. As he

sat down at the small breakfast table with coffee and milk and a plate of muffins, he said, “Last night you had a gun.” He reached for a warm muffin. “I want it.”

Chapter 9

Kadir handled Lexie's six-shooter in a way that assured Cassandra he was more familiar with weapons than she. He'd found the proper tools for cleaning the gun in a kit that was stored in the back of the hallway closet. Extra ammunition was stashed there, too, and he had gladly retrieved it. He'd very precisely and smoothly inspected and cleaned the six-shooter and loaded it. He was now examining the weapon once again.

As if he felt her gaze, Kadir lifted his head and looked squarely at her. She still wasn't accustomed to the smooth cheeks and chin, but she liked the look. Losing the beard changed his appearance drastically. Once his hair was cut, no one would recognize him.

Well, he'd likely need dark sunglasses to make the disguise complete. She'd recognize those eyes anywhere.

"You're staring," he said, only slightly accusing.

"Sorry. I've never before seen a diplomat who was so comfortable and capable with guns."

He shrugged and finished putting the weapon together. "I wasn't always a diplomat."

To be sure. Kadir was unlike any other ambassador she'd ever met, and since she had decided he was the one man in the world for her, should she ask for more details? On the one hand, he might feel such questions were too personal, not proper for a diplomat and his aide. He remained leery of her this morning, suspicious of her motives. If she pushed too hard, he was very likely to go off and handle this alone. She wanted to help; she needed to be involved.

But on the other hand, she wanted to know Kadir as deeply and completely as possible, and she didn't know how much time they had for such luxuries.

"You were a soldier?"

"Yes," he answered briefly.

"What made you decide to become an ambassador?"

The gun was reassembled, cleaned and readied to Kadir's satisfaction. He placed it on the table before him, and studied her with eyes that sometimes seemed to see too much. "If you really want to know, I'll tell you while you cut my hair."

They went into the hallway bathroom, which was slightly larger than the one off the master bedroom, and Kadir sat on the edge of the tub. Cassandra ordered him to remove his shirt, and he did. When that was done, she tossed a towel over his shoulders and began to cut. Cautiously, carefully, she cut his curling hair.

Just as she was about to prompt him to begin, he spoke.

"I had a sister," he said. "Her name was Amala, and she was three years older than I."

Kadir spoke of his sister in the past tense. That, and the tone of Kadir's voice, told Cassandra that Amala was dead. She thought of how hard it would be to lose one of her sisters. There was no need to tell him she was sorry, that she felt his pain. He knew.

"At the age of twenty Amala fell in love, but my father refused to give his permission for the marriage she desired. He arranged a marriage with a more suitable man, a wealthier, more powerful, more influential man. Amala didn't care for this man who was chosen by our father, but she had no choice but to do as was directed. That was the custom."

It was a barbaric custom, but she didn't point that out. Again, Kadir knew.

"Amala was a good daughter, so she married the man our father chose, and for a while she seemed content enough. Not happy. I don't believe I ever saw happiness in her after she was wed, but neither did I believe her to be unhappy. If I had known..." He took a deep breath and exhaled slowly. "But I did not, and it does no good to wish to step into the past and correct our mistakes. We can only move forward."

"That's true," Cassandra said gently.

"He killed her."

The news came without warning, and Cassandra flinched.

"Her husband caught her communicating with the man she had once desired to take as her husband, and he murdered her. He wrapped his hands around her neck and choked the life out of her, and crammed the letter she'd been writing down her throat. When that was done, he claimed that the taking of life was his due as husband to an unfaithful wife. As if to write a letter to an old friend was infidelity. As if Amala belonged to him, and it was his right to extinguish her life."

"I'm so sorry." Cassandra stopped cutting and laid her hands on Kadir's shoulders. Yes, he knew, but still she wanted to say the words to comfort him. He laid a hand over hers, briefly, and then dropped that hand as if it were not a good idea to touch her in even such a simple way. "That must have been very difficult for your family."

"Yes, it was. We wanted justice, but there was no justice for Amala. The taking of her life by a wronged husband was considered appropriate in the eyes of the law."

"What happened to him?"

For a moment Kadir was silent, and Cassandra cut a longish strand of hair. Her fingers brushed his scalp, ruffling newly cut curls and offering a bit of silent comfort.

"Nothing," he said softly as her fingers raked across the back of his head. "My father became ill and never recovered. He died a year later. My mother, whose joy died with her only daughter, passed away less than six months later. But Zahid went on as if nothing had changed. For him, I suppose nothing *had* changed."

"Zahid Bin-Asfour, the man who's trying to kill you?"

"Yes. There have been so many times when I've wished that I'd followed my first instinct and put a bullet in his brain when I heard the news. He left Kahani a few months after he murdered my sister, even though he had broken no law. I almost followed him. It would not have been easy, but I could have tracked Zahid down and killed him in such a way that no one would ever have known I did it. I was twenty-one years old, a soldier who believed that such vengeance was not only possible but just."

"But you didn't."

"No." For a moment he was silent, and Cassandra suspected he was finished, at least for now. And then he continued. "I wanted Zahid dead, but more than that I wanted the country I call home to be a place where such things don't happen. To transform the very customs of a people takes a long time. It takes handshakes and compromise and perseverance. Big changes don't occur with the pulling of a trigger…but there are days when I wish I had made that choice, instead of the one that brought me to this place in time." He squirmed a little, obviously uncomfortable. "It is no longer acceptable in Kahani for a man to take his wife's life as if she were a possession of no importance to be done away with on a whim."

"And you did that," she said in a lowered voice. "You brought about that change."

"Not alone, but I was there." Kadir became silent again, and this time he was truly done.

Cassandra decided not to push for more. She had questions, but he'd told enough of the story for now. She continued to cut his hair, snipping the strands shorter and shorter, watching as the short black strands curled gently.

"Someone in town might've seen something," Kadir said as she was taking a few last snips. "I'll go to town and listen to what the locals are saying."

"*We'll* go to town," Cassandra corrected. "Tomorrow would be better than today. About half the shops are closed on Sunday, and today the town will be crawling with investigators, anyway. Besides, you need to rest today. You're recovering very well, but your arm was cut deeply and you nearly drowned."

"I'll go alone. I don't wish to involve you in this," Kadir argued.

"I'm already involved," she said angrily. "In case you have forgotten, both of us might've been on that yacht when it exploded. If I had accepted your dinner invitation, we'd both be fish bait right now. Someone tried to kill me, and that means I'm definitely involved."

He turned his head and looked up at her. Wow, what a change a shave and a haircut made. Kadir looked not only younger, but was actually approaching pretty. "I've always known that my dedication to bringing change to Kahani might cost me my life. It's a sacrifice I'm willing to make. I am not, however, willing to sacrifice your life."

Cassandra didn't so much as pause before answering. "That's very nice, but I'm not staying here while you go to town on a fishing expedition of a different sort. I don't come to Leonia often, but I know people in town and they know me. If you want all the gossip, you have to be part of the in crowd. Or at least a sister to someone who's a part of the in crowd."

"But..."

"Besides, I know where the keys to Lexie's motorcycle are kept."

His eyes lit up. "Motorcycle?"

"Motorcycle."

"That is not a motorcycle!" Kadir insisted. "It's a motor *scooter!* And it's *pink!*"

"So?" Cassandra responded with a decided lack of outrage.

"How are we supposed to remain inconspicuous on a pink motor scooter?"

"Don't be a baby."

"A baby?"

Cassandra's smile wiped away almost every trace

of Kadir's outrage at the knowledge that his only mode of transport lacked power and was obviously made for a woman.

He'd taken her advice and rested most of the day yesterday. Sleep had claimed him often during the day. He hadn't realized how exhausted his body was, but Cassandra had known. She had recognized his weakness when he had not, because she knew him so well. How oddly disconcerting.

During the day she'd tended him often as he'd rested, feeding him, changing the bandage on his arm, touching him in casual ways that felt anything but *casual.*

Kadir was still determined to keep his distance from Cassandra. Last night he had attempted to sleep in the guest room, but when he'd awakened in the night he'd found Cassandra's body close to his. They both wore nightclothes, and the touching involved during the night was incidental and casual, but still…to sleep with her and not have her in all ways was a kind of torture.

She was still stunned and relieved that he'd survived the explosion that had been intended to take his life—and hers. He didn't want her to sleep with him because she suffered from a type of posttraumatic stress. That was the only explanation he could come to, since she'd denied him vigorously on Friday night and again on Saturday night, and then openly offered herself to him Sunday morning.

One day she would thank him for being so circumspect. Today was not that day.

"I suppose we could walk…." Cassandra began.

"No." Walking to town and back would be a waste of precious time. One commodity he did not have to spare was time.

They had a plan, of sorts. His role was to be that of a boyfriend who'd come from Silverton in the dead of night to comfort Cassandra after her close call. Kadir was to remain as quiet as possible while she pumped the locals for information. Even though he looked very different—wearing another man's clothes, with his hair cut short and his facial hair gone—his voice remained the same. Cassandra would ask the questions; he would listen. There should be no danger in today's excursion. Everyone thought he was dead.

She had taken one of his ancestor's names which was a part of his full name—Yusef—and shortened it to Joe. That's what she would call him, if introductions were called for. Joe, he of the pink motor scooter.

When they returned to the cottage this afternoon, she would make a call to the Kahani Ministry of Foreign Affairs and try to get a message to Sharif.

Sharif, who had loved Amala and probably still did. Sharif, who would gladly die before throwing in his lot with Zahid Bin-Asfour.

It would have to be an innocuous message, since they could trust no one else with the secret that Kadir lived. Not yet. They could only hope that Sharif would return the call.

Kadir scoffed at the ridiculous scooter, and took the helmet Cassandra offered. At least it wasn't pink, but instead was black. Hers, however…

Cassandra didn't immediately put the helmet on her head. She had something to say. At moments like this she was endearingly transparent, as if she had never known a moment of deception. Coming from a world where deception was a part of everyday life, this trait was one of the things he most admired about her.

"There's something I think I should tell you, even though I'm not supposed to tell you, or anyone else. It might have nothing to do with this, but I can't be sure." She wrinkled her nose, ever so slightly. "I just feel like you should know everything before we get started."

"I will keep anything you tell me in strictest confidence."

"I know, but...I've never shared proprietary information with anyone before." She looked at him with those amazingly intelligent and changeable gray eyes. "It feels a little like betrayal, but if I don't tell I might be betraying *you* and I can't do that."

"Anything you tell me stays here, in this shed." Morning sun slanted through the open doors, touching Cassandra's ponytail and making her glow with an unreal beauty. "I would never betray you in any way."

She hesitated, but not for long. "You believe that Zahid Bin-Asfour is behind the attempts on your life."

"I have no doubt," Kadir said.

Cassandra nodded, as if she understood. "It isn't widely known, but Prince Reginald met with Bin-Asfour just a few days before he was murdered. Investigators are trying to find out more about the meeting, in case it might have something to do with the prince's death, but no one's sure why they met."

"Drugs," Kadir said. "Zahid made a delivery, and he remained in the prince's company for several hours. Our own security council learned of the meeting weeks ago. Zahid makes much of his money through the sale of narcotics. Usually he does not participate in those dealings himself, but when royalty is involved..." He shrugged. "Illegal drugs were delivered to your prince in exchange for money or promises. I suspect there was more to the meeting than a simple sale, but it's likely we will never know."

Cassandra didn't chastise him for not sharing this information with her sooner. Instead she nodded, satisfied that he was armed with all the information she had to share.

"One more thing," she said, tucking the pink helmet under one arm and looking him squarely in the eye, in that fearless way she had. "Can I have a kiss for luck?"

He should say no and keep some distance between them, but this was one request he could not deny her.

As Cassandra had suspected, the village was buzzing with news of the explosion. Many people spoke of seeing the sheik on Saturday, never suspecting that before the end of the day he'd be blown to bits.

They were all anxious to talk to her, since she'd been with Kadir on his tour of Leonia. No one questioned her presentation of Kadir as "Joe," her silent boyfriend from Silverton. He didn't look like a sheik, in ratty hand-me-downs from Stanley—or one of Lexie's ex-husbands who'd left a few things behind. With the haircut and shave, and the dark glasses hiding his eyes—it was possible *she* wouldn't have recognized him if she hadn't witnessed the transformation for herself.

For the time being, she didn't even think about what she wanted from Kadir on a personal level. This was business, and she had always been able to throw herself into the task at hand at the expense of all else. She did that now. They didn't learn much, but apparently everyone in Leonia had been outside their homes and shops at the time of the explosion and had seen it firsthand.

It was late afternoon when the photographer from the

Quiz found Cassandra and Kadir sitting at an outdoor café, sipping coffee and comparing notes. Sadly, they had learned nothing that would help them discover who had been behind the explosion. A number of investigators from Silverton were still in town, questioning everyone who'd claimed to witness the explosion. They'd had all day yesterday to interrogate the citizenry, but since just about everyone in town claimed to have seen the explosion, the complete investigation would take days—perhaps even weeks. So far Cassandra had been able to avoid the investigators, but she knew they'd catch up with her sooner or later. She'd tell them the same story she'd told the local officer. That was the truth as she'd known it at the time, so it wasn't exactly a lie.

The photographer who had followed them to Leonia on Saturday very boldly walked up, introduced himself as Simon York and asked if he could join them. Then he sat before they had a chance to respond. Ignoring the insignificant Joe, he offered a hand across the table. Cassandra ignored the hand.

"What do you want?" she asked coolly.

"Now, don't be that way, Cassie. I know you're probably upset about that little picture in the *Quiz* last week, but I was just doing my job."

Since York had been ignoring Kadir, the photographer was surprised when a large hand shot out and grasped the wrist of the offered hand.

"She's Ms. Klein to you," Kadir said in a lowered voice.

"Sorry," York said. When Kadir released his hold, the photographer rubbed his wrist and frowned at Cassandra. "I didn't take you for the type who'd go for a thug."

"Joe's very protective," she said. "If you behave

yourself you won't have any problem with him. Now, why are you here?"

The photographer leaned onto the table, listing slightly away from Kadir. "I was taking shots of the sunset Saturday," he whispered. "I got a few perspectives that included the yacht. A man crept into the far right side of my view, but I wasn't worried about that. I figured if the photo was a good one I'd just crop him out. He stood there and watched until the yacht exploded, and then he turned away." York paused for effect. "He was smiling."

"You got a shot of his face?" Kadir asked.

"Yes." York clearly did not want to include "Joe" in the conversation, so Cassandra gave a little wave of her fingers, and Kadir leaned back in his chair to observe.

"Have you told the investigators?" Cassandra asked.

"No." York sounded horrified. "If I do they'll confiscate all the film. I can't have that, now, can I? It isn't as if knowing that man was watching will bring the sheik back, right? My developing lab is back in Silverton. I didn't want to wait, but I'm afraid if I go home I'll miss something here. There's no telling what might happen next! I left the film at the local photographer's shop. The old man there said he'd have them ready in—" York checked his watch "—a little less than one hour."

"Why are you telling me this?"

York smiled. "I just take pictures at the moment, that's true, and I love my camera. But I'm quite a writer, too. If I have the photographs and an exclusive interview with the woman who watched Al-Nuri ride out to his death, a woman who had been connected to him romantically in a previous story in the *Quiz,* I'll be set. My name will be made overnight." His grin widened. "I'll be a *star,* Ms. Klein."

The idea of giving this man anything repulsed her, but… "I want to see the photos as soon as they're available."

"Of course." York cut a suspicious glance to Kadir. "Does he have to come along?"

"Yes," Cassandra said, calling up a tone that left no room for argument.

York ordered his own cup of coffee, and he carried the conversation. He had spoken to the same people Cassandra and Kadir had interviewed. No one else had mentioned the man York had caught in his photograph. Still, once they had the picture in hand, someone would surely recognize him. This was a small village, and even though tourists came and went, they had to stay somewhere, and they had to eat. Someone in Leonia would remember him.

Simon York could already taste what it would be like to be a star.

A few minutes before the photos were supposed to be ready, the three of them left the café. Kadir remained protectively between Cassandra and York. He wanted the photos, but he didn't like or trust York. The distrust and dislike was clear on his transformed face.

York pointed. "There, just beyond the candy shop at the end of the next block."

A puff of black smoke danced from the area York indicated. It was curious, but not alarming. Then another puff followed, blacker and larger than the last one.

It was Kadir who began to run first, his long legs quickly picking up speed. He glanced back and shouted, "Fire!"

Chapter 10

By the time Kadir reached the photo shop, black smoke was drifting from the building in thick clouds, and people had begun to step out of the surrounding shops to see what was happening. On the sidewalk just outside the shop he removed the sunglasses and tossed them aside, took a deep breath to fill his lungs with air and then opened the front door.

Behind him, someone shouted that it wasn't safe to go into the building. With the door open, black smoke billowed out, wafting around and behind Kadir, alarming those who had gathered to watch. Again, someone shouted that they'd called the fire department and it really wasn't safe to go in there.

Kadir didn't retreat. The fire was growing quickly. If anyone remained in this shop, the fire department would likely arrive too late to be of any assistance.

Flames shot ominously from the back room. Kadir stared into the flames for a moment. If the photographs were in that section of the building, it was too late to save them. He glanced at the front counter, which was surrounded by smoke but not yet afire. If the photos were there, waiting for York to pick them up, he didn't see them...and there was no time to search.

An elderly gentleman lay facedown on the floor. It looked as if he'd been trying to reach the door when he'd fallen. Kadir kneeled down beside the fallen white-haired man and placed a finger at a fragile-looking throat. He found a pulse, weak and uncertain, but steady enough. Again, Kadir glimpsed into the fiery back room, wishing he had come here sooner, wishing he could get a glimpse of the man in the photograph, the man who had watched his yacht and all the people on it destroyed.

But the time for those wishes was gone; the film, the photographs, the negatives—if they were in that back room, they had all been destroyed. Kadir lifted the unconscious man off the floor, and as he did so he felt something warm and wet on his shoulder, where the man's head lolled. Blood, no doubt. Apparently this man had not been overcome by smoke, but rather had been bashed over the head so he could not escape.

By the man in the photograph? Almost certainly.

The rescue took mere moments. On the sidewalk the neighboring shopkeepers and customers gathered around. Seven people watched, and they all breathed in relief at the sight of the old man. Cassandra and the photographer hung back, watching expectantly.

"Thank you, sir," a plump woman wearing a chocolate-stained apron said as Kadir gently laid the injured man on the sidewalk, well away from the smoky entrance to the fiery shop. She touched gentle fingers to the bloody patch of gray hair. "Poor dear, did he fall trying to get away from the fire?"

"I believe so, yes," Kadir said, lying easily as he retrieved the sunglasses he'd tossed to the sidewalk before entering the shop. Cassandra had said they were a necessary part of his disguise, so he slipped them on.

All eyes were on him, and in the distance sirens wailed. The last thing he needed was to spend the rest of the day being interviewed and thanked. The investigators would expect a last name, and proof that "Joe" was who he claimed to be. It crossed his mind that he could run back into the shop for a few moments to search for the photos, but since the old man had been hit on the head—not accidentally injured trying to escape—it was certain the photos had been destroyed, or taken. "I wish I could stay but I must go. Please see to the old fellow until proper assistance arrives."

"Yes, of course, but..." As Kadir made his way toward Cassandra, the plump woman asked, "Who are you? William will surely want to know who saved him."

"My name is Joe," Kadir answered.

"Joe *who?*" a customer asked, raising her voice as Kadir increased his step.

"Just Joe," he called. He took Cassandra's arm and walked quickly away from the scene. "The pictures have been destroyed or stolen," he said in a lowered voice. He turned his gaze to the photographer. "Can you describe the man you saw?"

Distraught over losing his precious photos and chance at stardom, York sighed in disgust. "I suppose. But what difference does it make now?"

Kadir's patience was near an end. He could drag the annoying photographer into the nearest alleyway and force him to tell all he knew. He could, but he would not. "If you can lead me to the man who watched the explosion and then walked away with a smile on his face, I will give you an exclusive story that will indeed make you a celebrity. Everyone in Silvershire, and well beyond, will know your name."

"Why should I believe a thug like you?" York asked sullenly.

"If I were a thug, I could very easily beat the information out of you," Kadir said calmly. "You are small, and without an excess of toned muscles in your upper body. It would not be difficult."

For the first time, York looked at Kadir with analytical eyes. "Where are you from? Not Silverton, I'd guess."

Kadir glanced at the little fellow. "An exclusive, in exchange for everything you know about the man you saw."

"Sure, *Joe.* Why not? What have I got to lose at this point?"

They made two more turns, and found themselves on a narrow, deserted street. There York stopped. He leaned against a quaint stone building and began to give a description. Kadir listened carefully. Most of the information was useless. The man was of average height, appeared to be Arabic, dressed in an expensive black suit and was clean-shaven.

"That's it," York said with hands offered palms up. It was an expression of total surrender. "Now, what about my exclusive?"

"After I find him," Kadir said as he took Cassandra's arm.

"What?" York followed them down the sidewalk. "That wasn't part of the deal."

"How do I know you told the truth?" Kadir asked. "You do not strike me as being the most scrupulous of men. When I know what you told me was true, then you'll get your story."

"Who are you, anyway?" the small man persisted. "You're no *boyfriend,* I know that much. You're not from Silverton, either, I'd wager, and English is not your first language. A spy, maybe? That in itself will make for interesting reading. Sexy Secretary Spotted in Company of Stupid Spy, or something along those..."

Kadir moved fast, spinning, catching York by the throat and pressing him against the nearest stone wall.

"Sorry about the stupid thing," York croaked. "I'm just..." He struggled to take a breath. "Come on, give me something, man. I lost all my pictures. You can't blame me for being in a bad mood."

Kadir leaned in close. "If you ever again write a word about Ms. Klein without first obtaining her permission, you will regret it." He lowered his voice. "And she's not a secretary."

He released the small man, and this time when Kadir and Cassandra walked away, York did not follow. When they were several steps down the unevenly paved street, Kadir took Cassandra's arm. She listed in closer, and he was undeniably relieved and glad to have her body so close to his.

But now was not the time for such a simple pleasure. "I believe the man York saw worked for me."

Kadir wasn't sure that the man York had seen was one of his employees, but he suspected it might be true.

After all, how many well-dressed Arabs had been in Leonia on Saturday evening? No one had known they were coming here, and only the one photographer had followed. Still, he did not want to discuss the matter until he had more information. Cassandra tried to do her own calculations. Average height—that ruled out Jibril and Haroun, who were both very tall. Clean-shaven—not Sayyid or Hakim. Who did that leave? Tarif, Fahd and the crew she had never met.

Would anyone from the yacht's crew dress in a suit?

She also had to consider that the man York had seen might've shaved that very afternoon, and perhaps his idea of average height was not the same as her own. In truth, they had eliminated no one.

Cassandra called the Kahani Ministry of Defense and left a message for Sharif Al-Asad—who was not available. The message had to be simple, and could not even hint that Kadir was alive. Cassandra left the message that she was a friend of Sheik Kadir's and would very much like to speak with Sharif to relay her deepest sympathies on the loss of his friend.

She left the phone number to Lexie's cottage with a surly man, hoping that Sharif would return her call. She wasn't at all convinced that the message would be passed along.

Dinner was soup without conversation. Kadir was lost in thought, occasionally frowning and always distant. He was understandably distraught at the possibility that the assassin was one of his own, and just as distraught that he could not identify the culprit. Tomorrow they would go to town once again, and this time the questions would be different. More specific.

But for tonight they needed to rest and wait for a phone call that might or might not come.

Kadir settled on the couch to watch the evening news. His assassination was still a major story, even though two days had passed since the explosion. Better tidings were also shared, once the announcer had passed on the fact that there were no leads as to who might be responsible for the sheik's assassination. Princess Amelia was expecting a baby. Lord Carrington and his wife had been trying to keep that bit of intelligence a secret for a while longer, but someone in the know had leaked the story.

Someone in the know was always willing to leak this story or that. Simon York would be devastated that he'd missed yet another scoop.

Cassandra sat next to Kadir, and when the news turned to insignificant weather and local interest, she leaned into him. "There's nothing to do now but wait," she said.

"That's true," Kadir said in a lowered voice.

"You might as well relax tonight." Her fingers traced the bandage beneath the fabric of his shirt. "I should probably change your bandage."

"It's fine," Kadir said absently. "The cut is healing nicely."

She sighed and laid her head on his shoulder. It was very nice, just to sit this way—close and connected and warm. But it wasn't enough, and Cassandra had decided that Lexie's way could not be her way.

"I've been trying to seduce you for almost two days, now, and my efforts have been wasted," she said bluntly.

"Cassandra, don't—"

"Let me finish, please."

She took his silence as agreement.

"It's not surprising that I'm a failure as a seductress,"

she admitted. "Hints and flirting and girlish smiles are not my style at all. I prefer to be direct in all matters, and perhaps I should be direct in this one, as well."

She slipped one possessive arm around Kadir's midsection. "I've never held a man like this. I've never kissed a man the way I've kissed you, I've never cuddled and kissed and felt as if my heart was about to burst out of my chest. Until the night you were injured, I'd never slept with a man, not in any sense of the word." She took a deep breath and made the big confession. "I'm a virgin."

Kadir sighed. "All the more reason—"

"You said I could finish what I have to say without interruption."

Another sigh. "Proceed."

This was better than hints and not-so-subtle brushes of her hands on Kadir's body. This was not a game; it was her life. "For as long as I can remember, I've been waiting for something special. A feeling. A bond." She might as well say it. "Love."

She felt Kadir's body stiffen, but she didn't release her hold on him, and he didn't push her away.

"My mother always told me that the first time she saw my father she knew he was the one for her. Her heart fluttered, and her stomach flipped over and she *knew* in an instant. I've waited for that feeling since the age of fourteen, Kadir, and when I saw you walk off the plane..."

"Don't," he whispered.

"I felt it for you," she continued. "Maybe what I feel is purely physical and in time it will pass, fading away or simply disappearing. Maybe it's more than physical, but in the end what I feel and what I want won't matter. I don't know. Maybe I'm not supposed to know. Maybe I'm just supposed to accept what I feel and trust that what comes is meant to come. All I know is I want you, and you have become annoyingly determined to fight me at every turn."

Kadir placed a hand in her hair. "You fought against any attraction for me from the moment I first saw you. When you changed your mind so suddenly, what was I supposed to believe? More than anything, I don't want to hurt you. I don't want you to regret a moment of our time together."

"I've been fighting my feelings for you since that first moment because you didn't arrive in the way in which I'd always imagined." It was an embarrassing admission. "The arrival of love should be neat and tidy, or so I thought. I should meet a suitable man—*the* suitable man—at a social function or on the beach, at the market or in the museum as we both studied the same painting." It all sounded silly now. Who could plan their life to the last detail? What was life without a few surprises? "It shouldn't arrive in a way which forces me to choose between my career and the love I've always wanted. Love should be neat, I decided, not messy and complicated. So I pushed the flutter aside and dedicated myself to my work, and tried very hard not to like you too much.

"And then I watched the yacht explode, and I knew that to set aside something so special and extraordinary was a mistake." She rose up slowly and laid her mouth on Kadir's neck. He tasted so good, and she wanted this and more. "Enough explanation. I want you to make love to me. If that doesn't happen, if I turn my back on something so exquisite, it will be like passing by a beautiful flower and not taking the time to smell it, or closing my eyes when a breathtaking sunset appears because I know it won't last. If you really and truly don't want me,

I'll understand. But I think you do." She laid her hand over the erection that strained his jeans. "I think you do."

Kadir's arms encircled her, and she knew that tonight he wouldn't deny her. "I can make you no promises beyond tonight, Cassandra. We don't know what tomorrow will bring."

"I'm not looking at tomorrow. Just tonight. I waited for you, Kadir, I waited a long time. I don't want to wait anymore."

He threaded his fingers in her hair, held her head gently and kissed her. Deeply and completely, he kissed her. One hand slipped beneath her T-shirt and then simply laid there against her skin as if he were trying to absorb her. Could he feel her heart pounding? Could he feel the rush of blood that made her lightheaded and shaky?

She had used the L-word, but Kadir had not. Maybe he didn't love her at all, but wanted her in a purely physical way. Maybe he was afraid of love. It didn't matter. She didn't want to pass up this beautiful moment in the name of keeping her life neat and tidy.

Life wasn't supposed to be neat and tidy, and it took this crisis to teach her that fact.

With a suddenness that startled her, Kadir drew away, ending the kiss. "I wasn't thinking." He moved a strand of hair away from her face, and let his fingertips trail against her cheek. "I don't have any form of birth control with me, and I suspect you don't, either. Leaving you carrying my child is a chance I won't take."

Kadir didn't mention that there was a madman out to kill him. He didn't mention that nine months from now he might be dead, or fighting his battles on the other side of the world. He didn't have to.

Cassandra reached into the back pocket of her borrowed jeans and pulled out a condom that crinkled in its package. "My sister has a box of these under the bathroom sink. Will they do?"

Kadir sighed, in what seemed to be relief, and took the condom from her. "Yes, they will do."

Kadir slipped the condom into his own back pocket, for now. What Cassandra thought was love would soon prove to be purely physical, as she suspected it might. Still, he did not want her to regret revealing her deepest sentiments to him.

Even when they went their separate ways, when she returned to her job and he returned to his—if he survived—he didn't want her to regret this.

Kadir unfastened and unzipped Cassandra's jeans. Every move he made was slow, deliberate. His fingers raked across the sensitive, pale skin of her belly, and she trembled. She was so soft. So delicate. More than anything, he did not want to hurt her. He lowered his head and kissed the sensitive flesh, letting his lips linger there for a moment. Kadir didn't take much time to revel in those things in life which were fine, those things which made life worth living. The love of a beautiful woman, even if it was not meant to last, was certainly one of those things.

Cassandra's thighs parted slightly, in a purely instinctive move, and her eyes drifted to a sensual half-closed state. The gray of her eyes was soft now, as soft as the wings of a dove and filled with what she believed to be love. With every stroke of his fingers, with every brush of his lips, the desire in those expressive eyes grew to a new height.

Kadir pulled Cassandra's shirt over her head and tossed it aside, and while she was in that vulnerable state, half-undressed and flushed with desire, he drew her body against his and kissed her deeply. Her mouth met his with hunger and anticipation and desperation. She knew as well as he did that this relationship was temporary. Even in the best of circumstances, they came from two very different worlds. She was a modern woman; modern women were not welcomed in his country, not even now.

No, this was a passing alliance, one that could not last, but it was also deeply meaningful. Cassandra meant more to him than a short-lived liaison, but he couldn't tell her that. Unlike her, he had to guard his innermost thoughts. He could not afford to be so brutally honest, as she had been.

In a matter of minutes, he could take her here on the couch, quickly and fiercely joining and making love to her. Her body trembled, her heart pounded and she was ready in all ways. Kadir had been ready for this woman since the moment he'd seen her, but now…now he wanted her with an unexpected intensity. He had never wanted any other woman quite this way.

But Cassandra had shared everything with him, and he knew this was her first time. Her first time should not be fierce *or* quick. It should be memorable, and those memories should make her smile and shiver for a long time to come.

Her bra was easy to remove with a flick of his fingers and a gentle plucking, which removed the lacy fabric from her breasts. When the undergarment had been tossed aside, he lowered his mouth to take a nipple deep, and Cassandra arched her back and gasped. The sensation was a new one for her. New and powerful and delightful. Her fingers settled in Kadir's newly shortened curls, and she pulled him closer. He drew her deeper into his mouth, then pulled back and traced the hard nipple with the tip of his tongue. She sighed and shuddered, and he slipped his fingers into her opened jeans.

Pushing her jeans down over her hips, he slipped his fingers between her legs. There she was hot, wet and quivering. He touched her, teased her, aroused her with his mouth on her neck and breasts and his fingers stroking until she was rocking beneath him in a gentle and instinctive sway, trying to draw him closer, deeper.

She whispered his name, her body shook and Kadir rose up to take her mouth with his. His tongue speared into her mouth while his fingertip just barely entered her eager body. Her gasp of surprise at the new sensations caused her entire body to jerk. He kissed her, and one finger brushed against a sensitive nipple while another moved inside her.

Cassandra climaxed with a cry and a lurch, her body undulating against his as the orgasm made her entire body quiver. He held her, and reveled in the release as if it were his own. Even as the tremors faded and she relaxed, she continued to kiss him. The kiss turned gentle. She was satisfied, for the moment.

The way she touched his body told him she would not be satisfied for long. One hand settled over his erection and moved languidly.

"Oh, my," she said when she was capable of speech. "That was definitely worth waiting for." She smiled at him.

Kadir's heart lurched at the sight of that passionate

grin. He dismissed the reaction to one of pure, unsatisfied lust and that wandering hand.

"To bed?" Cassandra said in a soft voice that spoke volumes.

"Yes," Kadir said, drawing away from her and caressing the perfect, half-dressed body she presented to him. Had he ever seen anything more beautiful? Had he ever wanted anything so much?

He promised himself at that moment that even when morning came, Cassandra would not be sorry she'd waited for him.

Chapter 11

There was a new and almost palpable energy in the atmosphere, as if a storm was coming. The very air Cassandra took into her lungs felt different, as if it had been charged with electricity. She'd wondered earlier if she might be shy if the evening progressed as she'd planned, but she was not. There was such joy in making love, there was no time for shyness.

She and Kadir undressed one another as they made their way to the bedroom and the bed, and like the kissing, each and every move seemed very right and natural. Buttons, zippers, the occasional awkward move to rid oneself of an unnecessary article of clothing—it was all as natural as taking a deep breath of the electrified air.

Heaven help her, at the moment she needed Kadir the same way she needed air and the beat of her heart. He was that important, that necessary.

Together they slipped beneath the covers, and Kadir's naked body rested against and then pressed against hers. Legs entwined, and arms encircled. They were so close, so near to coming together in all ways.

He wrapped his arms around her and kissed her, gently and then deeply, as if they were just beginning again. Oh, the feel of his bare body against hers was heavenly. That sensation of skin to skin was a delight in itself, as sensual and exquisite as any touch could ever be.

They kissed and touched, and reveled in the friction of one body against another. Kadir's erection pressed into her hip, but he didn't seem to be in any rush. Time moved very slowly, so that every kiss, every caress, was elongated. Savored. Cassandra's body reached for something new and untasted, but like Kadir she didn't rush. She allowed him to lead her, to guide her in this new, sensual experience.

Kadir touched her with his fingertips, as if learning each of her body's curves and swells. Shoulder, neck, breast, the soft skin above her belly button, the crook of her elbow. He watched the sight of his hand against her skin, by the light of the moon that shone through the bedroom window, as if he felt the same wonder she had discovered.

She watched his face, when she could, wondering at the beauty and mystery of this night, wondering if she truly knew the man behind that handsome face. She did more than look, of course, enjoying an exploration of her own. She traced Kadir's newly shaved jaw, which was sharp and masculine, and then she pressed one hand against the well-muscled chest and feathered her fingers through his short, black curls while pulling his mouth to hers for another, deeper kiss.

After much kissing and touching, she felt bold enough to wrap her fingers around his erection, to stroke and explore and arouse. Kadir's response was to growl low in his throat and roll her onto her back. He swiftly put on the condom and spread her thighs with his knee, and she awaited the joining she wanted so badly. But Kadir didn't immediately give her what she wanted. Instead he touched her, he traced her with his fingers and slipped one finger inside her again.

He was making sure she was ready in all ways. He was thinking of her, even now.

"It's time, Kadir." She wrapped her legs around his hips as he guided himself to her and slowly, very slowly, pushed inside her waiting body. She held her breath, savoring and wondering and, yes, worrying a little. Kadir wasn't accustomed to inexperienced women, she knew that. Would he be disappointed in her? She wanted him to experience the joy that overwhelmed her. There should be no disappointment in this night.

When he was fully and completely inside her, every worry danced out of Cassandra's mind. Her body had already begun to tremble in anticipation. Ripples of pleasurable sensation flickered through her.

Kadir began to move slowly, tenderly, and she moved with him, her hips rising and falling, her heartbeat racing. Her body had not only adjusted to accept his, it welcomed him. They fit together perfectly, in a way that surely no other two people ever had, or ever would. He had been made for her, and she had been made for him.

She quit thinking while he made love to her. Her instincts took over completely, and she found herself holding on, rising higher in order to take him deeper, and they found that rhythm that took them beyond all questioning, all worrying. There was just this, and for now that was fine. It was very fine.

Cassandra gasped and held on to him as the sensations grew, and then she shattered, crying out as the orgasm washed through her body with a force she had not expected. Kadir came with her, his body stiffening and lurching as he drove deeper than before.

Everything slowed, and eventually she was able to breathe again. Her body was exhausted, in a new and entirely wonderful way.

What she felt at this moment, it was so powerful it must be love. What else could fill her heart this way? What else could make her feel as if the entire world had changed just for the two of them? She wanted to tell Kadir that she loved him, but since she had already mentioned the L-word once tonight, and he had not, she decided to leave it alone. For now. If love was meant to come, she suspected there would be no stopping it.

Kadir rolled away from her and headed for the bathroom to dispose of the condom. If he was going to be around for a while, she might want to see about some other form of birth control, something that wouldn't come between them or require that momentary delay. It was unlikely he would be around long enough for her to address that concern. She dismissed the worry from her mind because she didn't want anything, not even thoughts of the future, to spoil what they had tonight.

Very soon, Kadir slipped back into bed, large and warm and naked, and he pulled her body against his. He was silent for a moment, and then he whispered, "Are you all right?"

He was worried about her because this was her first time, because she had been a virgin.

"I'm fine," she said, and then she laughed lightly. "No, I'm more than fine. I've never felt so absolutely wonderful in my entire life."

"Good." Kadir sounded relieved.

They found a comfortable position where arms and legs linked and bodies fit together, and very soon Cassandra fell into a slumber so deep it was unlike any other she had ever known. All was right with the world; her world, at least. It was the dreamless sleep of a well-loved woman.

Kadir remained awake long after Cassandra's breathing fell into the deep, even breathing of sleep.

Cassandra was a beautiful, sensual woman, and he had wanted her beneath him for what seemed like a very long time. Still, he had attempted to be prudent where she was concerned, knowing their future was not only uncertain, it was nonexistent.

Her talk of flowers unsmelled and sunsets unseen had undone him and all his prudence, but that wasn't the only reason he'd so gladly taken her as the lover she'd asked to become.

Betrayal from within had always been a possibility, and still he was greatly disquieted by the possibility that the person responsible for the explosion that had taken many lives had been a comrade, if not a friend. A part of him wanted to believe that York had seen one of Zahid's soldiers, a terrorist who had somehow managed to follow Kadir and his party to Leonia and plant the explosive.

But that was not logical. Logic insisted that the assassin had come to Leonia *with* Kadir, and that he'd had an opportunity to plant a bomb because he was welcomed on the yacht.

Tonight he had allowed himself to dismiss logic and

hide inside Cassandra, for a while, to lose his fears and his anger in her in a way that was undeniably magnificent. She thought what she felt was love, but she'd soon enough discover that was not the case. What she felt was physical. Women often confused the needs of the body with the needs of the heart. Kadir did not.

But this was nice. He liked to feel her lying beside him, to watch her smile and moan and touch with the amazement that can only come with something new and beautiful. Cassandra and all she offered, however temporary, might very well save his sanity while he searched for the truth.

The truth would not be easy to find, but if Zahid had been involved in Prince Reginald's murder, then the proof was likely here, in this country. Uncovering the facts of Zahid's involvement would help them all. Cassandra would be a hero for solving the mystery of the royal assassination. Simon York would get his damned exclusive.

And Kadir would be able to turn the entire world against Zahid Bin-Asfour and his followers. Fostering a primitive culture was one thing; assassination was another entirely.

He would be in this country for a while longer. Days, perhaps weeks. In that time, he would gladly keep Cassandra as his lover. He admired and liked her, he was intensely attracted to her, he enjoyed her company. But before he left, she had to understand that this was no more than any other short-lived affair. They could comfort one another, they could find pleasure and companionship in this bed. But when it was over, it would be well and truly *over.*

She did not belong in his world, and he had no place in hers.

* * *

Kadir had half expected a visit from the police sometime Monday night. He'd given his name as Joe, after pulling the injured man at the photo shop from the fire, and several people had seen him leave the scene with Cassandra. It wouldn't exactly be difficult to make the connection, since they'd been all over town that morning and he'd been introduced a dozen times as her boyfriend.

But no one came looking for Kadir, or Joe. No one arrived to question Cassandra, either. She didn't understand the why of that, not until she received an early-morning call from Ms. Dunn.

The older woman almost always appeared to be tough and uncaring, but she did care, in her own brisk way. Her frequent calls were intended to make sure Cassandra was all right, and during Tuesday morning's call—a call which awakened Cassandra from a sound sleep—Ms. Dunn asked pointedly if the investigators had dropped by the cottage to ask questions. Cassandra assured her boss that since the evening of the explosion, no one had questioned her about what she'd seen.

"Good. I told the investigators that were dispatched to give you a few days to recover from the shock," Ms. Dunn said, apparently relieved. "The local police have your statement, and that's sufficient for now."

"Thank you." Cassandra glanced over at Kadir. He was awake, but still drowsy. He didn't look as if he'd slept well. "I could use a few more days to myself, and it isn't as if I can tell the investigators anything I haven't already told the local officers."

"Precisely," Ms. Dunn responded. "You can certainly have a few days. I would like to have you back in the office by the weekend," she added. "Next Monday at the very latest. The week before the gala is always hectic, and I'll need you here." Once again, the tone was sharp.

"Of course," Cassandra answered, having no real idea when she might return to the ministry.

When the call was done she closed her eyes. It was early, the sun was barely up, but she didn't expect sleep to return. She was well rested, but also languid. Maybe they could stay in bed and make love all day. It was a nice idea.

Kadir pulled her close, as if his thoughts mirrored hers. He nuzzled her neck and cupped one breast in a warm, large hand. Long fingers rocked and danced over her skin. That easy, familiar touch made Cassandra feel as if she were literally melting.

"Good morning," he said, his voice deep and slightly gruff.

"Good morning." Cassandra smiled. He was seducing her all over again—not that she actually needed to be seduced. His hands already seemed to know her body well, and she responded to him without taking the time to think about the whys and the shoulds, the why nots and the should nots. She just enjoyed. In fact, she reveled.

She raked her fingers along his back, his side, his hip. Caressing him this way was much easier than she'd thought it would be. There had been such a steady wall between her and the opposite sex until she'd met Kadir. She knew very well how to keep men at a distance; she'd been doing that for years. Now she was learning how to draw one in, and in spite of her inexperience she didn't think she was doing too badly.

If she thought too much about what she was doing, she might find reasons to stop. So she didn't think. She touched, and kissed and whispered.

She more than half expected Kadir to roll her onto her back and push inside her. After all, there were condoms on the bedside table, not so very far away. But he didn't reach for one. Instead, he sighed and rolled away from her, leaving the bed altogether.

"Much as I would like to spend the day in bed," he said, "we have work ahead of us today."

"I'm rather tired of working," she confessed.

Naked, aroused...beautiful...Kadir stopped at the bathroom door, turned slowly and grinned at her. And her heart did all sorts of unexpected tricks in response.

"It would be too easy to spend the day in bed with you," he confessed. "Much too easy." The grin faded. "It would, in fact, be very easy to remain dead. To become Joe and have nothing in the world to do but love you."

Love in the physical sense, Cassandra knew without being reminded.

"It would be too easy, Cassandra, to hide here with you. But that's not who I am, so this morning I will take a cold shower and go to town without you. You should stay here and rest. Sleep a while longer. Think only of pleasant things. Let me deal with the unpleasantness of the world, just for today, while you rest here."

Kadir went into the bathroom and closed the door behind him, and a moment later Cassandra heard the water begin to run. And a few minutes after that, she slipped from the bed and joined him. They didn't have time to waste, she knew that. He wanted her; she needed him.

Today she would not allow Kadir to shower alone, any more than she'd allow him to take on the unpleasantness of the world without her.

* * *

For someone who'd been a virgin yesterday, Cassandra was quite insistent about what she wanted. Insistent, and persistent and unfailingly determined.

He had given her what she'd wanted when she'd joined him in the shower. How could he not? Afterward she had insisted on coming with him to the village once again. This time he had argued more strenuously—for all the good it had done him. If Sharif called, he would leave a message or call back, she'd argued. If the police stopped by to question her—or him—wouldn't it be best that she not be there? If they were going to keep their stories straight, then they really should stay together.

None of those arguments had swayed Kadir, but Cassandra knew how to get what she wanted from him. She'd asked the question…

What if the man who blew up your yacht and started a fire in the photo shop comes here and I'm alone? What will I do, Kadir?

It made no sense for the man who'd attempted to assassinate him—the man who had killed many innocents on the yacht in order to get to Kadir—to go after Cassandra. But there was also no guarantee that he would not.

Kadir parked the pink motor scooter not too far from the ruined photo shop—and just a short walk from Simon York's room at the small, nearly ancient Leonia Inn. The inn was four stories tall, narrow and near crumbling, but it was the cheapest hotel in town. Kadir was hoping to get to the inn without seeing anyone who might recognize him, but the plump woman he had seen outside the photo shop yesterday saw him and rushed from the candy shop to intercept him. He tried to ignore her, but she waved and shouted his false name.

"Joe!" Pudgy fingers wiggled on her outstretched arm. Her run was an effort, and there was much jiggling as a result. "Joooooe!"

On the sidewalk, he and Cassandra stopped and turned to face the woman. He never should've given her a name yesterday when she'd asked, not even a bogus one.

The woman slowed down considerably when she realized that Kadir and Cassandra were not going to run from her. "Thank goodness I saw you," she said in a loud, gasping whisper. "You really should know…" She stopped to catch her breath.

"Know what?" Kadir asked as the plump woman came to a stop before him. Today she wore a name tag on her chocolate-stained apron. *Mary.*

"It was very clear to me, and to the others, that you didn't wish to speak to the police. I don't know why." Mary sounded slightly disapproving. "But you did a good thing, Joe, and we decided it wasn't right that a good deed should bring you trouble. So, Henry told the officer who questioned us that he saw the smoke and pulled William out of the shop before the flames got out of hand. William was unconscious, so he can't very well dispute the fact."

"Who is Henry?" Kadir asked, amused and relieved.

"Henry is the red-haired fellow who was in my shop yesterday when all the ado took place. He's a regular customer," she added with a touch of pride. "He can't get enough of my toffee."

"There were several witnesses," Cassandra said.

"Yes, but none were tourists. We all agreed that it would be best if Joe didn't have to…well, we're grateful that William was saved, and no good deed should bring a man unwanted attention. We all agreed."

"I take it William has regained consciousness?" Kadir asked, leaning slightly forward in anticipation. "Did he see anyone? Does he remember how the fire started or…" How much did Mary and the others know? "Does he remember anything at all?"

"Not a thing," Mary said in a no-nonsense voice. "He smelled smoke, turned and then he apparently fell and hit his head on the counter."

If that was what William remembered, then that's what everyone would believe. Everyone but Kadir, at least. "I'm very glad that your friend is well." He took Mary's hand, bowed slightly and then kissed her knuckles. "Thank you, and many thanks to your friends, as well. I very much appreciate your discretion." When he rose up again and looked at the candy maker's face, she was blushing. Her cheeks were an outrageous shade of red.

"It was nothing, really," she said, breathless once again. "I just thought you should know."

"The fire was contained to the photo shop?" Cassandra asked.

"Yes, luckily. None of the adjacent buildings were damaged, since no one shares a common wall with William's shop. I have complained many times about keeping kids out of those narrow alleyways, and keeping them clean is always a chore, but today I'm grateful the alley between my shop and William's is there."

"I'm very glad to hear that no one else suffered damage," Kadir said.

The candy maker waggled a finger at him. "You should stop by and try my toffee when you have the chance. Skinny girls like your girlfriend here don't eat much candy, I understand that, but a strapping young man like yourself doesn't have to worry about a few extra calories."

No one had called Kadir a young man in a very long time, but he supposed *young* was relative. "I will most definitely stop by and purchase some of your fine toffee."

Again Mary blushed.

They said goodbye, and once again Kadir and Cassandra headed for Simon York's inn.

Just before they reached the doorway that would take them into a dimly lit and sparsely furnished lobby, Cassandra laughed.

Kadir held the door open for her. "What is so funny?"

She took his hand as they stepped inside the inn. "If you expect to pass yourself off as a Joe, you're going to have to work on the accent, and for goodness' sake, stop being so charming."

"Charming?"

She squeezed his hand and her grin widened. "No one named Joe kisses a woman's hand quite the way you do."

Chapter 12

It was obvious to Cassandra that Kadir didn't care for Simon York. She didn't, either, for that matter. He'd hounded them, after all, and was responsible for that embarrassing photo that had gone into the *Quiz*. But it was possible the annoying photographer had knowledge they didn't, so for now the three of them were working together.

At the moment Kadir was speaking, and York furiously scribbled notes in a small tablet. The man wanted his exclusive—one way or another—and he listened to Kadir's words as if there might be gold hidden among them.

"Did you know," Kadir said solemnly, "that Zahid Bin-Asfour and Prince Reginald met not long before the prince's assassination? Three days before, to be precise."

"Yes, of course I knew that," York said. It was an obvious lie. The sparkle in his beady eyes and the way he hurriedly scratched the information on his paper told Cassandra that much.

"Bin-Asfour delivered illegal drugs to the prince," Kadir continued, "but we don't know what, if anything, he received in exchange. Do you?"

"I can find out," York promised. "The *Quiz* has people everywhere, and I do mean everywhere. If anyone knows what went on between the prince and Bin-Asfour, we can find it."

Cassandra felt a decided shimmer of unease. If anyone in the ministry ever found out she'd been a party to handing this kind of information to an employee of the *Silvershire Inquisitor,* she'd be out on her ear in a heartbeat. Ms. Dunn had never been known as a forgiving woman.

"Very good," Kadir said. "I expect you will get the investigation started immediately. Until then, it would be best if we keep the information about the meeting under wraps."

York's head snapped up. "Under wraps? Are you kidding me? This is hot stuff. I can't keep it to myself!"

Instead of arguing, Kadir smiled. "Hot stuff? I thought you said you already knew about the meeting." He shrugged, very casual and uncaring. "That is up to you, of course. I imagine once this bit of information becomes public knowledge, everyone will be scrambling to find the rest of the story. I thought it might be best if you waited until you had everything, but if you want to divulge what we have thus far…"

"No, no," York said, very grudgingly agreeing. "This had better pan out, mate. The princess is preggers, and I could be in Gastonia snapping photographs."

"You and every other photographer in this part of the

world," Kadir argued. "I thought you wanted to be different. Special. A star among celebrities."

"Yeah, yeah," York mumbled.

Cassandra was still stuck on "The princess is preggers." It would make a typical *Quiz* headline.

"Now—" Kadir leaned back in his chair and stared at York "—what can you tell me that I do not yet know?"

Kadir dominated the small rented room Simon York called home, not only with his size but with his energy and his force of will. No matter where he went, no matter how crowded or sparsely populated a room might be, how could every eye not turn to him? How could any person he spoke to not give his every word their full attention?

No one would ever mistake him for a Joe for very long, no matter how diligently he worked to lose his accent and his charm.

Cassandra wished fervently that he *was* a Joe. That they could date for a few months, and spend weekends here at the seashore or down in Barton. He'd ask for her father's blessing, in a few months—maybe a year—and then they'd be married. At night they would each talk about their day, before falling into bed to make love. They could live in Silverton, where she'd continue to work until the babies came. Maybe even after the babies came. Wouldn't he be wonderful with babies?

But he wasn't a Joe and never would be. Dammit.

Before the meeting was over, York promised to do some discreet digging into the meeting between the prince and Zahid Bin-Asfour. This new research would require a trip to Silverton, as he did not feel secure in sharing too much information over the telephone. The three of them planned to meet here, in this room,

Thursday evening. By that time York was sure to have something of importance to share.

At least they could hope that would be the case.

Cassandra was certain Kadir would immediately head back to the cottage, once the interview with York was done. But he didn't. Instead he walked around town, his movements slow but his eyes sharp. He studied tourists and shopkeepers with equal intensity. Once she even caught him staring at a man and his children with what might be called melancholy. Perhaps it was only her imagination, but she was sure she saw some emotion on his face. It took her immediately and completely back to that insane moment when she'd decided he would be a wonderful father…and wasn't that an unusual bit of fancy for her to indulge in?

He even stopped at Mary's shop and bought some toffee, with cash he borrowed from her, as he was presently without funds. The woman was thrilled to see him, and was equally pleased to sell him a small container of her special candy.

Kadir remained lost in thought as they walked back toward the scooter. For the most part, he'd been silent as they'd walked about town, but now he mumbled to himself. He even cursed.

"What are you talking about?" she asked as he reached for his helmet.

"I don't have any idea if he's still here, so why do I waste my time looking into every café and alleyway?"

"Who exactly are you looking for?" Kadir knew the men in his entourage very well. Surely he suspected one—or more—over the others.

He shook his head. "I don't know. I still don't want to believe that any of the men who worked for me would do such a thing. If indeed I was betrayed from within my own household, surely the traitor has left."

"But you're not *sure.*"

Instead of answering, Kadir leaned over and gave her a quick kiss. "Maybe he's waiting for my remains to be discovered. Zahid is not a trusting man. He might very well insist upon concrete proof of my death."

"But you don't know that."

"No," Kadir said.

"Who do you think might've..."

He shook his head and mounted the scooter. She climbed on behind him and held on.

"I refuse to speculate on the possibilities," Kadir said. "Logic aside, I very much hope I'm wrong in my suppositions, and the man who tried to kill me is a stranger who left Leonia soon after the explosion took place."

Cassandra raked her hands against Kadir's midsection, in an instinctive offer of comfort. She didn't know what to say. Heaven above, she always knew what to say, in any situation, no matter how awkward. It was her job to know what to say!

But this was Kadir, and she loved him. She wanted to protect him from what he saw as the only logical explanation. While she searched for words, he lifted her hand and kissed the knuckles. Then he put the scooter into motion, and the time for speaking words of comfort or support was gone.

The afternoon was a long one. The phone only rang once, and it was a call from Piper Klein, who wanted to know if her daughter was well. It was touching to think that those who knew Cassandra well believed she'd be devastated by the death of a man she barely knew. But then again, women seemed to understand one another in a way men did not.

Sharif did not call. Would another message from Cassandra so soon be too much? Would someone question why she was trying so desperately to contact Sharif? Kadir decided it was too soon for another message. It would only draw attention to her, and he didn't want that.

She sat next to him on the couch, close. Very close. Her thigh brushed his, and that simple touch was enough to make him hard.

"What do we do now?" she asked, as if she had been reading his mind.

"We wait."

She fidgeted, very slightly. He had a feeling she did not *wait* well. "Maybe we should go back to town and directly ask people if they've seen the man who was photographed. We do have a vague description, thanks to York, and we can visit the shops nearest the pier and…"

"No," Kadir answered sharply. If he asked the villagers about identifying a man who was supposed to be dead and they verified that he had indeed been seen, would they all be in danger? Would Mary the candy maker and William from the photo shop and the employees at the market close to the pier all be targets for a man who would surely prefer to remain among the dead?

If Kadir was right in his presumption, of course, and if the traitor was still in Leonia. Neither of those was certain. "We will wait for York to return and see what sort of information he can give us."

"That's two days, Kadir. What are we going to do for the next two days?"

That was one question he could easily answer. He

kissed her, and she yielded quickly beneath his touch. One of her delicate hands rose up and touched his hair, and her lips parted.

He'd never known a woman like Cassandra Klein. In his country women were not allowed the kinds of freedom what would produce a wonder like her, but it was more than that. In his duties as ambassador he had been around the world. He had spent time with women from all cultures. He had even slept with more than his share.

But Cassandra was special. No one else had ever been able to draw him in so closely, so intimately. Not intimately of the body, but of the spirit. It was as if she were inside him, all the time. It was as if he had known her forever, as if they had shared more than a few precious days.

When the time came, leaving her would be difficult. Fortunately, now was not the time for thinking about leaving.

She slipped her fingers into the waistband of his jeans, teasing him with her incredible softness and the bold warmth in her touch, and he forgot everything but the physical. He wanted to be inside her. He wanted to feel her quiver and hear her make those sounds low in her throat. He wanted to hear her cry out his name as she reached orgasm.

Kadir tried not to think about the importance of her being a virgin before last night, but he could not entirely push that knowledge away. She had waited for him. For *him,* and no one else. He didn't want her to regret a moment of their time together, even when it was over and they were living their lives thousands of miles apart.

They undid buttons and zippers while they kissed,

neither rushing nor dawdling, but moving slowly and without hesitation toward what they both wanted. Cassandra was wonderfully responsive to his touch. Kadir saw her response in the way she moved, in the flush that rose to her skin, in the swell of her breasts and the change in the way she breathed. And he saw it in her eyes, gray and soft and so full of spirit that the gaze alone touched him in a way nothing, and no one, ever had.

Before he removed her jeans, she reached into the back pocket and withdrew a condom. She had come to him prepared, and he was glad. Tonight he didn't want to stop. He didn't want to call even the shortest halt to the progression of their lovemaking.

Cassandra insisted that he be as naked as she, and soon he was. She touched him boldly, with delicate fingers that drove him beyond all rational thought. He wanted her around him, and nothing else mattered. Nothing.

Soon she reclined on the couch and drew him to her, her long legs wrapped around his hips, her eyes closed and a small smile teasing the corners of her mouth. Kadir just barely began to enter her, and then he stopped.

"Look at me," he whispered.

Cassandra did as he asked and opened her eyes. Dove-gray eyes so soft and desirous and loving, they touched his heart. Kadir was determined that his heart not be involved in this. Even if it was, even if he could not stop what he knew was impossible...he could never tell her. He could never tell anyone.

Their eyes were locked as they came together. Cassandra's body quivered. He adored that quiver, the sigh, the way she lifted her hips to meet his, in a rhythm that came so naturally to her. In her arms, in her body, he forgot everything and everyone else. There was nothing in the world but pleasure and beauty. There was nothing in the world but Cassandra and the way she came to him.

She climaxed quickly, almost as soon as he was fully, deeply inside her. Kadir did not wait, but joined her in a moment of pure, powerful release that wiped all the ugliness and uncertainty of the world away, for a short while.

As soon as she caught her breath, Cassandra laughed lightly. Kadir lifted his head and looked down at her. Light from the lamp at the end of the couch shone down on her exquisite face.

"What's funny?"

"Me," Cassandra said. "Us," she whispered in a lowered voice. "I didn't know sex could be so furious and wonderful and unstoppable. Like a freight train." She laughed again. "The bed's not so far away, and yet it seemed as if it was, when going there meant moving my body even a fraction away from yours."

Kadir lowered his mouth and kissed her throat, so slender and pale and soft. "I want you in every room of this house," he whispered.

"It's a small cottage," she responded, her fingers teasing his hair. "And we already have the master bedroom, the master bath and the main room covered. That just leaves three rooms."

He lifted his head and looked down at her. In this light, with that expression on her face, she was the most beautiful creature he had ever seen. A woman like this could very easily steal a man's heart away.

Her fingertips touched his cheek. "Kadir, I…"

He saw the expression in her eyes, he felt the weight of what she was about to say in the very air around them.

So he kissed her to stop the words from leaving her mouth. He wanted Cassandra to the depths of his soul, but he could not allow love to come between them.

Wearing Lexie's pajamas, Cassandra sat at the desk in the main room, where just a couple of days ago she'd found a six-shooter. Kadir had that weapon now. It was never far from his hand.

A tradition was a tradition, no matter where she happened to find herself. It was Tuesday night, after all. Lexie's only stationery was plain white and lined, but it would do.

Dear Mum,

Lexie's place is beautiful, and very relaxing. I didn't realize how much I needed a holiday until I was forced to take one. The sound of the waves is unexpectedly soothing, and there are moments when the sight of the sea takes my breath away. No wonder Lexie loves it here.

There was no need to let her mother know that Kadir was alive, not yet, and if Piper Klein knew there had been fires set and assassins spotted, she'd be here in a matter of hours. Mothers were like that, almost-psychic or not. It was definitely best that her parents remain in Barton.

I'm feeling much better than I was just yesterday.

And how.

You were right. You and Lexie and Daisy and Paula, you were all right. Bet you never expected to hear me say that. But it's true. When you told me to enjoy my life instead of planning it so carefully, when you told me that not everything can be planned to the last detail like an itinerary for a visiting dignitary, when you said I needed to enjoy my life, you were all right. Some things can't be taught, they have to be lived, and love is one of those things. Loss, too. The sheik and I became good friends in his short time here, as you suspected. Nothing anyone could've told me would have prepared me for the sight of Kadir's yacht exploding before my very eyes and the devastating emptiness that followed.

Even though she'd learned just a few hours later that Kadir hadn't been killed, that moment would haunt her forever.

I'm much better, now, truly I am. Ms. Dunn wants me back in the office by the weekend. There's always so much to do in preparing for the Founder's Day Gala. Will you and Dad be making the trip to Silverton this year? I can get you tickets to the gala, but Dad has to wear a tuxedo. Tell him I said the tux he wore when you were dating won't do. The ruffles are disturbing, and it hasn't fit him well in years.

The gala was an exclusive event, but as an employee of the foreign service, she could always manage to wrangle a couple of extra tickets, if need be. As far as her father was concerned, nothing ever went out of style, and if an outfit was a little tight, well, as long as it covered everything that needed to be covered, he felt it was just fine.

He had not always fared well living in a house full of fashion-conscious women.

When I write next Tuesday's letter, I'll be back in my apartment and life will be back to normal.

She didn't know if she'd be home by next Tuesday or not, but expected she might be. Once Kadir had his answers, he'd be gone. As for normal, well, she didn't think any part of her life would ever be the normal she had come to expect. Still, she'd learn to manage. She wasn't the type to fall apart when things didn't proceed as she wished. She was, after all, a realist.

Would losing Kadir when he walked away from her be any less painful than watching the yacht explode? Of course it would. She wanted to know he was alive and well, that he breathed and smiled and maybe even went fishing. Somewhere in the world.

But it would be painful.

See you soon, I hope.
Love,
Cassandra

Eventually her mother would learn that Kadir had survived the assassination attempt, and there would be plenty of explaining to do. But those explanations were not necessary tonight.

Letter written, Cassandra turned off the main room lights and crawled into bed with Kadir. He seemed to be asleep, but she didn't think he was. She placed her body close to his, and draped one arm across his torso. She would miss this holding as much as the sex, when he was gone.

Was that why Lexie always found another man so

quickly after her romances failed? She knew what it was like to be held and cherished and loved, and that had to make the loneliness sharper, more painful.

Cassandra wasn't sure how she'd adjust to sleeping alone, once Kadir was gone. She was smarter than her eldest sister, though, and she knew he could not be easily replaced. Kadir could never be replaced.

The timing of Kadir's quick, deep kiss on the couch, earlier in the evening when she'd still been trembling from making love, had reminded her that he didn't want her to tell him that she loved him. It was a complication he didn't know how to handle, and she understood that very well. So she wouldn't tell him again. He knew, and that was enough. It would have to be. She would take what she could get from this short-lived relationship and store it all away in a glorious memory that would never fade.

Memories were a poor substitute for the real thing, but if it was all she could have then she'd make it be enough. Her body trembled, and she pushed away the acute pain that threatened to rise to the surface. She hadn't known, all those years she'd waited for her true love to arrive, that she wouldn't be able to keep him forever.

Chapter 13

Cassandra was willing to drive the pink scooter into Leonia Wednesday morning to post her letter. It would be a short enough and safe enough trip, she imagined. Kadir didn't plan to do any more investigating, not until after York returned—hopefully with some new information—so there was no reason for him to go with her. She was very aware that with every appearance in town, Kadir took the chance that someone might recognize him. Try as he might, he wasn't a very good Joe.

Still, he refused to allow her to go to town alone. Since just yesterday she'd argued that they should not be separated, she didn't fight him on the matter for very long.

There was no reason to tarry in the village today. She mailed her letter, Kadir bought a larger supply of toffee, which he said was quite good, and then they headed back to the cottage.

It did not escape her attention that while they were in Leonia, Kadir once again kept a sharp and curious eye on the people around them. It was as if he suspected every man woman and child in town of being a potential assassin, and she couldn't blame him for that. He carried Lexie's six-shooter, but it was well concealed. If she hadn't known where he carried the weapon, she wouldn't even realize it was there.

It was also apparent to her, as they ran their errands, that in spite of her concerns the townspeople were fooled by their cover story. They truly believed that Kadir was her boyfriend from Silverton, come to comfort her. *Boyfriend* was such an inadequate word to describe their relationship, but when they held hands and he leaned in to whisper in her ear, she imagined that's just how it appeared to onlookers.

She looked forward to a quiet day at the cottage. A quiet day and a half, to be precise, since York wouldn't return until late tomorrow. She and Kadir could make love in every room of the cottage, and then they would start all over again. They could fish in the afternoon, and maybe Kadir would make love to her on the rocks—though she did wonder if the rocks were too hard and sharp for that activity. Only one way to find out, she supposed. She'd cook for him, and make him laugh, and ask questions about the life she would never get to share, and do her best to make him forget all his troubles—for a while.

She had a day and a half to make enough memories to last a lifetime.

Cassandra and Kadir entered the cottage through the kitchen door. She glanced around the cozy room, wondering where and how, exactly, Kadir planned to make love to her here….

Before the door was closed, Kadir grabbed her hand and yanked her down and behind him, at the same time dropping the tin of candy and smoothly drawing the six-shooter. Cassandra grabbed on to the denim of his jeans in order to steady herself, and peeked around his leg to see what had startled him. A man stood in the door between the kitchen and the hallway, his own gun drawn and steady.

The gunman had olive skin, like Kadir, and long black hair that was mostly pulled back in a ponytail. A few strands escaped and framed a harsh, thin face. His beard was untended, and that, along with the narrowed eyes, gave him a wild and decidedly dangerous appearance.

Kadir almost immediately relaxed. "You startled me," he said as he returned the weapon to its proper place.

The armed man who had broken into the cottage while they'd been in Leonia lowered his own weapon—which was a much more modern gun than Lexie's six-shooter—and cocked his head to one side. "Kadir?" The man's voice was truly puzzled, but after a moment's study he grinned. The smile changed his face entirely, and he wasn't quite so scary. "You're alive."

Kadir assisted Cassandra to her feet as the armed man strode into the kitchen. When she was standing, brushing off imagined crumbs from Lexie's kitchen floor, the bearded man stepped past scattered pieces of toffee and threw his arms around Kadir, laughing—not quite maniacally.

When the laughter and the relieved hug ended, Kadir placed his arm around Cassandra's shoulder. "This is Sharif Al-Asad, assistant to the Kahani Minister of Defense and my oldest friend. Sharif, this is Ms. Cassandra Klein, the aide I was assigned upon my arrival in Silvershire."

Cassandra offered her hand, and Sharif shook it briefly. "A very pretty aide, if I may say so." His eyes were appraising, and she imagined Al-Asad realized that she and Kadir were involved. Eyes like that didn't miss much. Sharif didn't have bedroom eyes, like Kadir, but those eyes were sharp as a hawk's, and unfailingly apprising.

"You didn't return my call," she said, only slightly accusing.

"When my oldest and dearest friend is assassinated, you expect me to sit in an office and reply to telephone messages?"

She looked Sharif Al-Asad up and down. His beard and his hair needed tending, but his clothes were expensive and fit him well. He handled his pistol with the ease that came with years of experience. He was, she knew instinctively, indeed a dangerous man. "I suppose not."

This was the man Kadir trusted. The only man, he said. As the three of them walked into the main room to share the happenings of the past few days, a chill walked up and down Cassandra's spine.

Kadir might trust this odd man with his life, but she did not.

Sharif's smile faded as he watched Cassandra walk into the kitchen. When his old friend had asked if she could make him a cup of hot tea, Kadir had realized that he wished to speak alone.

"We can leave now," Sharif said, standing nimbly. "We'll walk out the front door while she's in the kitchen, and I'll have you to a safe place within two hours. When you're secured, I'll return to Leonia to personally conduct the investigation."

Kadir did not stand. He reached up and laid a stilling hand on Sharif's forearm. "I'm safe here, for now."

A touch of sharp anger crossed Sharif's face. "You have known that woman for a *week,* and you're willing to place your life in her hands? I have never known you to be a fool, Kadir, but that is a decidedly foolish decision. Zahid might've bought her, or blackmailed her, or threatened her. She could poison you at any time, or shoot you while you sleep, or…"

"She would do none of those things."

"You have no way of knowing that with any certainty."

But he did know, in a way that would be difficult to explain. "She thinks she loves me," Kadir said with a sigh.

Sharif's features softened a little. "It could be a game…."

"This is no game."

"You've been blinded," Sharif said as he reluctantly sat once again.

"I didn't say that I love her." Even if he thought he might, one day, love was impossible in these circumstances and it was a useless exercise to even consider such a thing. "I do like her, very much."

"That's clear enough," Sharif grumbled.

Kadir actually smiled. "I like her well enough to protect her while I can, and I certainly like her well enough to walk away when I'm finished here." There was no need to point out that as long as Zahid lived, no one Kadir dared to care for would be safe.

While Cassandra was busy in the kitchen, Kadir told Sharif of his suspicions. Sharif was surprised, but not shocked. Nothing had the power to shock him anymore; he had seen too much. Still, he was as disturbed as

Kadir that someone who'd been within the tight circle might've been behind the explosion. A phone call this afternoon would get an investigation into everyone who was thought killed on the yacht into motion.

"We have discovered why Zahid came here to meet with Prince Reginald," Sharif said once plans for the new investigation were complete.

Kadir awaited the rest, an eye on the doorway Cassandra would walk through, his ear partially tuned to the sound of her work in the kitchen.

"Zahid offered an alliance," Sharif continued, contempt clear in his voice. "An allegiance between Silvershire and Bin-Asfour in exchange for all the recreational drugs the prince desired."

"And the prince's response to this ridiculous offer?"

Sharif shrugged his shoulders. "That we do not know. If the offer was rejected, then Zahid would have felt it was within his rights to kill the prince. I have a man on the inside, and in a few days..."

"You have someone within Zahid's camp?"

Sharif nodded. "My informant has been disillusioned, but realizes if he tries to walk away from the organization he and his family will be killed." Again, that shrug. "If he's caught sharing information he should not he will surely be killed, but that's a risk he's willing to take."

Before Cassandra was finished preparing the requested tea, Sharif left the cottage by way of the front door. He was not one to sit still and wait, and if there was even the smallest possibility that the culprit remained in Leonia, he wanted to be on the watch. Sharif did not leave the cottage without a soft warning for Kadir to take care, and a suspicious glance toward the kitchen.

Cassandra returned to the main room with a tray

bearing three cups of steaming tea, along with sugar and cream. She searched the room quickly, looking for their guest, and Kadir informed her that Sharif had departed.

With a sigh that spoke of relief, she placed the tray on the coffee table and sat beside him—close, as she so often chose to do. The expression on her face said it all. "I don't trust him."

"Why not? He wants Zahid dead as badly as I do. Maybe more. He's the one man in the world Bin-Asfour can't buy or blackmail." He thought again of Sharif's assertion that Cassandra herself might've been bought, and he dismissed it just as quickly. She could've killed him a hundred times in the past four days.

No, the danger Cassandra presented had nothing to do with Bin-Asfour.

She wrinkled her nose as she considered his assertions. "Your friend strikes me as a man who knows no boundaries. He'd do anything to get what he wants, including sacrificing you. You say he wants Bin-Asfour as much as you do, and I believe you. Let me ask you this. Would Sharif give his own life to take down Bin-Asfour?"

"Without doubt," Kadir answered.

"What makes you think he values your life more than his own? Maybe Sharif would be willing to sacrifice *you* in order to gain Zahid's trust, if it meant getting his hands on the man."

"Perhaps," Kadir answered softly, and more thoughtfully than he'd intended. With each passing year, Sharif seemed more desperate, more hungry, as if he had begun to realize that the man who'd murdered Amala might never have to pay for his crime.

"He doesn't like me at all," Cassandra said as she leaned snugly against his side.

No, his lover and his friend did not like each other. Sharif saw the potential for danger in Cassandra, and she saw the potential in him. Kadir supposed that no one or nothing in his life was entirely safe, but that was no way to live. He didn't want to spend the rest of his days looking over his shoulder and expecting the worst even of those he cared about.

Better to take a chance now and then than to completely close himself off from the few real joys of life. "Life is never entirely without risk."

Cassandra scoffed at that, but maybe she agreed because she did stop arguing.

That was fortunate, as they had better ways to spend the afternoon than in argument.

The next day and a half were everything Cassandra had hoped for, and more. She and Kadir made love and they fished and they laughed. They laughed a lot. They had late-night conversations about their childhoods and their siblings, their hopes and their fears, telling the sorts of secrets lovers share. They held hands and kissed often.

The only unwelcomed interruption came in the form of Kadir's scary, hairy friend, Sharif, who dropped by on occasion, usually appearing in such a way as to startle Cassandra. It didn't take long for her to realize that he did that on purpose. When Sharif was present, he and Kadir whispered to one another, sharing secrets they did not want Cassandra to know.

Fortunately Sharif never stayed at the cottage for any length of time. He came and went as he pleased, but he never remained in their company for very long.

On the Thursday evening scooter ride to Leonia, Cassandra held on to Kadir with all her might. Their time together was almost over. She knew it; she felt it to her bones as the wind whipped past them, and the smell of the sea filled each breath she took.

She'd expected to be in on the meeting with Simon York. Whatever he had discovered—if he had discovered anything at all—might actually have something to do with solving Prince Reginald's murder. She'd likely be forgiven anything—even lying about Kadir's death—if she could play a part in solving that mystery. Ms. Dunn would still disapprove, but she would offer forgiveness much more quickly.

But Kadir didn't lead Cassandra to the front door of the Leonia Inn. Instead he took her hand and they walked a narrow alleyway that led them to a deserted courtyard. There, Sharif waited. Kadir's friend was no more glad to see her than she was to see him.

Kadir spoke to them both in a tone of voice that left no room for argument. This was the voice of a high-level diplomat, a man who was accustomed to having his every order obeyed without question. "Sharif, I want you to escort Ms. Klein back to Silverton. Stay with her until I tell you otherwise."

Sharif's response was curt. "No."

Kadir's response was in Arabic, and spoken so quickly and so softly Cassandra didn't have a chance to understand what was said. She only heard one word she could decipher. *Amala.*

Panic welled up inside her. She didn't want to be sent away…she wasn't ready to say goodbye…. But when Kadir took her by the shoulders and looked into her eyes, she saw goodbye.

"Listen to Sharif, and stay safe."

Cassandra was incensed on so many levels, she didn't

know where to start. "I don't need an escort, a body-guard or a babysitter."

"I do not agree."

"I'm not a child, Kadir, and I don't appreciate being treated like one." So many emotions danced within her, she didn't know what to feel, what to say. "If anyone needs Sharif's assistance, it's you."

"I need no assistance."

"You're planning something, I can see it. What are you up to?"

He kissed her on the forehead lightly, as a friend might. "You'll know soon enough, and I don't want you anywhere near me when it happens."

"That does not sound good, Kadir. Not at all."

He smiled at her, but the smile died when Sharif began to argue with him once again. Again, Sharif spoke in Arabic, but this time his voice was loud enough and slow enough for her to translate easily.

Sharif didn't want to leave Kadir any more than she did.

Her heart beat too hard. This could be it. This could be the last time she saw Kadir. Whether he lived or died, whether Bin-Asfour succeeded in killing him or not. She'd lived safe all her life, and she was tired of living safe. Life is not without risk—everyone she'd ever loved had told her that.

"I love you," she said, speaking quickly so Kadir didn't have time to stop her. "I waited all my life for you, and now you're just going to walk away from me as if none of it matters?"

Sharif quickly took himself out of the circle, moving several steps away and pretending to search the alleyway for interlopers or eavesdroppers.

"You only think you love me," Kadir argued in a

lowered voice. "That happens, sometimes, when sex is involved. Women don't seem to be able to separate the heart from the physical act of love, when in truth the two usually have little in common."

The pain cut to the quick. Was there nothing but sex between them, after all? "Do you love me, just a little?" she asked.

Kadir brushed a strand of hair away from her face, sighed and said, "No, I don't love you at all. I like you. I wish you well. I will carry the memory of these past days with me until the day I die, whether that happens tomorrow or fifty years from now." He looked her squarely in the eye. "But I don't love you, Cassandra. Please understand."

Tears stung her eyes, but she refused to shed them. She would not be an overly emotional, needy girl. And if she had to cry, she'd save it for a time when she was alone. But she did feel she could argue with Kadir.

"You could be a gentleman and…and…*lie.*" She'd convinced herself that he did love her, but maybe this was nothing more than she'd suspected all along. He'd needed a woman to warm his bed, and she was convenient. It wasn't as if she hadn't known that was possible the entire time they'd been together.

And still, it hurt. Everything hurt.

"Goodbye, Cassandra." Kadir kissed her hand, much as he had the candy maker's, and then he turned his back on her, leaving her in the company of a man she did not like at all.

The way Sharif took her arm and all but dragged her away indicated that he felt the same way about her.

The heaviness of heart was unexpected, as was the undeniable sadness that welled up inside Kadir on a wave as unstoppable as those in Leonia Bay. It would be easy enough to dismiss his distress as the effect of what he was about to do, but he could not lie to himself any longer. He could lie to Cassandra, and had, quite well. But he should not lie to himself.

If everyone he loved was not a target for Zahid, if he thought he could protect her, if he believed that they had even half a chance at a happiness that would last more than a few days, then things would be different. Things *could* be different. But all that was nothing more than a few fanciful wishes, and he was a grown man who had put aside such indulgences long ago.

At the Leonia Inn, Kadir ran up the steps to the third floor, deciding to forego the rickety elevator in favor of the upward jog that helped him to release some of his unexpected emotion—or should. The run didn't seem to help much, as he'd thought it might. Lately nothing was as it should be.

York answered Kadir's knock anxiously, glancing around for Cassandra as Kadir entered the room.

"Did you discover anything of interest?"

"Not a lot," York confessed. "Apparently Zahid Bin-Asfour and Prince Reginald met several times during the six months before his murder. From what I've been able to discover, it was nothing more than two men of like interests sharing drugs and women. An elite party, you might say."

There was more, but if York had not discovered the rest on his own, Kadir would not tell him.

"Now," York said, "about my exclusive."

York would get his exclusive, even though he had provided scanty information that would not prove to be useful. "Is there time to get a story in tomorrow's edition of the *Silvershire Inquisitor?*" Kadir asked.

"If it's hot enough, yes."

Hot enough. An apt enough description.

Kadir stood and gave the little man a well-practiced bow. "Sheik Kadir Bin Arif Yusef Al-Nuri, Director of European and American Affairs for the Kahani Ministry of Foreign Affairs, very much alive and at your service."

Chapter 14

On Friday morning, Cassandra took great care to prepare herself for a long day. Makeup disguised the fact that she'd not slept well, and while nothing could be done for the redness of her eyes—crying much of the night would do that to a girl—all things considered she didn't look too bad.

Her suit was expensive—one of her best—and it was perfectly cut. The dusky blue was a good color for her. Maybe her face did look too pale against the darkness of the suit, but she doubted anyone at the ministry would notice or care.

She could lose herself in work. There was much to do, as Ms. Dunn had pointed out more than once in their telephone conversations in the past week. It wasn't as if she'd ever actually believed that anything lasting could come of her affair with Kadir.

Sharif insisted on driving her to work. Since they'd left Lexie's cottage in his rental car after collecting the few belongings she'd had there, he hadn't said more than half a dozen words. But he had been attentive, rather like an ugly but dedicated guard dog. He did not take no for an answer, and he never led her to believe that she was, in any way, in charge of this operation. He refused to so much as discuss Kadir with her.

In front of the ministry, he searched the parking lot with sharp eyes. As she opened the door and stepped out he said, "Act surprised."

Cassandra leaned into the opened passenger door. "What?"

"You know nothing," Sharif said sharply. "You are shocked at the unexpected news, just as everyone else is sure to be."

"I have no idea what you're talking about."

"It's what he wants. Remember that."

Confused and annoyed, Cassandra slammed the passenger door. As she walked into the ministry building, she shook her head. Sharif knew English, she knew Arabic and yet half the time she had no idea what he was talking about.

As she walked into the office, all heads turned in her direction. She'd expected curious stares, but this scrutiny was more intense than she'd imagined. How on earth would she handle all the questions that were sure to be thrown her way?

Before she'd taken three steps into the office, Ms. Dunn bellowed her name.

Cassandra stepped quickly toward the director's bellow. What now? All week Ms. Dunn had been kindly and concerned about the situation, but there was no kindness in the voice that filled the ministry and had some employees staring at Cassandra as she passed, and others cowering at their desks as if nothing unusual was going on.

Cassandra walked into Ms. Dunn's office with her head held high. "You wish to see me?"

Ms. Dunn's answer was a hard-eyed glare, as she tossed the newest edition of the *Silvershire Inquisitor* onto her desk, front page screaming, Sheik Kadir Lives!

Cassandra's knees actually wobbled, and suddenly Sharif's parking lot warning made sense. Act surprised? There was no acting involved, at the moment. Why hadn't Kadir told her what he planned to do? Why had he left her in the dark?

She all but collapsed into the chair that was reserved for those employees Ms. Dunn interrogated, and she reached for the paper. When she spoke, she said, very softly, "Oh, dear."

"You didn't know," Ms. Dunn responded in a significantly lowered voice.

Cassandra lifted her head, and all she could do was offer a meek shake. She opened the paper fully. Kadir had actually pushed the news about the princess's pregnancy to the bottom half of the page. There was a photo of Kadir with his hair cut and his beard shaved, and he held a copy of the Leonia newspaper, which was dated several days after his reported death.

She scanned the article York had written. Kadir said he'd been wounded—and that was true enough—and that he'd found a remote home where he'd taken the time to heal. Also mostly true.

And then he said that he planned to return to the Redmond Estate on Saturday morning, where he'd wait until a new security detail could be dispatched from Kahani. He ended by stating that he still wished to meet with Lord Carrington as soon as the man returned to the country.

"Stupid," she whispered.

"What did you say?" Ms. Dunn asked.

Cassandra lifted her head and looked Ms. Dunn in the eye. "I said, *stupid,*" she repeated angrily. "There have been two attempts on his life since he arrived in Silvershire, and he's just told everyone where he'll be this weekend, and he's also informed the assassins that he has no security detail." She felt a heat of real anger rise to her cheeks. "That's incredibly foolish."

"Yes, well, I'll make sure there's local security at the estate until his own bodyguards arrive."

Would it be enough? Cassandra suspected not. Kadir was setting himself up as bait, hoping to catch the man who had betrayed him.

Ms. Dunn was much more relaxed, now that she believed Cassandra had not lied to her. "Would you like to resume your duties as aide to Al-Nuri?"

Cassandra almost said yes, but caught herself in time. Kadir had made his wishes clear. He didn't love her, and he didn't want her involved in this new, foolish scheme. She'd be better off staying far, far away from the Redmond Estate. And him.

And as far as Ms. Dunn or anyone else knew, Kadir had allowed her to believe he was dead for the entire week. No self-respecting woman would pick up where she left off as if nothing had happened. "I think not," she said coolly. "His English is almost perfect, so no knowledge of Arabic is necessary. Anyone from this office will be sufficient to assist him."

"Good. I'll send Timothy to the Redmond Estate in the morning, early enough to greet the sheik."

"Timothy is a fine choice. I'm sure he and Sheik Kadir will get along quite well."

In fact, Kadir and Timothy Little had nothing at all in common. They'd likely get on one another's nerves from the moment they met. That was not her problem—not anymore.

Cassandra stood, her knees much steadier than they'd been when she'd first sat down. Instead of surprise or worry, what she now felt was anger.

"Would you like to take this copy of the *Quiz?*" Ms. Dunn asked, pushing the newspaper toward her.

"No, thank you," Cassandra answered coldly. "I have no desire to read the article again."

Ms. Dunn would assume Cassandra's animosity was the result of Sheik Kadir not contacting her about his survival instead of telling his tale to a reporter. Cassandra didn't care what Ms. Dunn assumed, at the moment. The anger was very real.

As she left Ms. Dunn's office, the receptionist flagged Cassandra down. "Your mother's on the line for you."

Cassandra sighed. Talking to almost-psychic Mum would only make her feel worse. All that foolish talk about love and taking risks had made her vulnerable. Her mother would ask questions she couldn't answer—not yet.

This is exactly what she'd been trying to avoid in setting love aside. She hurt, and she'd been forced to lie to her boss and now she was supposed to lie to her mother, as well?

"Tell her I'm busy and I'll call her back," Cassandra said as she headed for her desk, hoping to lose herself in work, as Ms. Dunn had suggested.

And why not? Her work was all she had.

* * *

The Redmond Estate seemed too large and too cold, after his time at the cottage in Leonia. It had nothing to do with the size of the rooms or the view beyond the windows, Kadir knew. The estate was cold because Cassandra was not here.

But that was for the best, since *here* was not safe.

Kadir swept into the estate early Saturday morning, calling upon every ounce of arrogance he possessed. He sent the staff away, ordering them on a forced vacation. Kadir told the estate employees that he wanted time alone on the heels of his ordeal, but in truth he wanted them all out of harm's way. Most of them were elderly and would only be a hindrance if Zahid fell for his trap. Oscar took the rejection especially hard, wondering what he'd done wrong.

There were official representatives from Silvershire who were determined to act as bodyguards, as well as a small man with a tinny voice who had been dispatched from the Ministry of Foreign Affairs to take Cassandra's place. The small man, appropriately named Little, was easily intimidated and even more easily dismissed. The security guards were tougher to be rid of, but Kadir did manage to toss them out of the house and off the grounds, insisting that if they did not accede to his wishes it might cause an incident between their two countries. Eventually they, too, departed, though he imagined they'd keep a close watch on the estate.

By Saturday evening he was alone in the large house. Alarms had been set—not that he expected any security system would stop Zahid Bin-Asfour. The photographers had wandered off shortly after dark. Slipping into the estate would not be all that difficult, even with the security system on. Turning the system off would make it much too clear that Kadir expected company.

Kadir kept a number of weapons close by, including Cassandra's sister's six-shooter. It was by far the least sophisticated of his weaponry, but he felt a fondness for it, just the same.

The hours dragged by. He had been alone in the past. At times he had treasured those few times when he was truly and completely alone. But tonight he simply felt desolate. He had grown accustomed to the voices of others in his circle. Most of all, he had grown accustomed to Cassandra.

Sitting in a darkened room of the deserted estate—the office he had claimed as his own on the second floor—Kadir allowed his mind to wander.

Maybe if he caught Zahid, maybe if he killed the man who had threatened his life on many occasions—maybe then he could indulge in a private life. At the moment, he could not imagine a private life that did not have Cassandra Klein in it.

What would she think of Kahani? Would she find peace in the villa by the sea, as he did? Would she join him in his quest for change? To marry a woman from Silvershire and ask that his countrymen and coworkers accept her would not be easy, and yet…love was universal, and in Cassandra there dwelled all that a woman could be if she were offered the right opportunities. She was the living, breathing embodiment of what he wished to bring to his country.

Kadir sat in the dark for hours and waited for an attack of some kind of come. A bomb, a bullet, a knife in the back. The estate had been under surveillance, so another explosion was unlikely, as there had been no opportunity for a bomb to be planted. No, since the first two attempts had failed, he expected this one would be conducted face-to-face. With any luck, he'd see the attack coming and get off a few shots first.

Without luck—he was as good as dead.

Cassandra's anger toward Kadir had bled over to his friend Sharif, who'd known all along what was going to happen. Their conversation about the situation had been short and without satisfaction, since Sharif was no more happy about the plan than she was.

For once, they actually agreed about something. That agreement was not at all comforting.

Sharif didn't want to be here, she knew that, but he refused to leave—even when she ordered him to do so. He'd followed her to the market this morning, sullen but ever present. Since returning to her flat, he'd split his time between pacing the halls talking to himself and pacing in the kitchen, drinking the incredibly strong coffee he'd made in her machine. No wonder he didn't sleep!

After a long Saturday of shopping, cleaning, doing laundry and worrying, Cassandra ate a salad in her kitchen for dinner before settling onto the couch to watch television. Well, the television was on. She didn't pay much attention to what was on the screen. Sharif was in the kitchen, pacing, drinking coffee *and* talking to himself. Now and then she picked up a word she could decipher. *Stupid. Dangerous. Nonsense.* Apparently some of his thoughts mirrored her own.

When her mother called—not for the first time today—and started to leave an almost panicked message on the answering machine, Cassandra picked up. She'd put this conversation off for two days, and she supposed it was time to get it done, as best she could.

At first, Cassandra allowed her mother to rant. Piper Klein was worried, after all, and rightfully so. It was a mother's privilege. Cassandra didn't say much. In the end she told her mother she was fine, and that she really didn't want to talk about Sheik Kadir and what had happened. Not yet. She couldn't lie to her mother the way she had to Ms. Dunn and everyone else at the ministry, not even by allowing assumptions that were untrue. It was for that reason that she'd avoided talking to her mum for so long. So she told her mother that she simply could not discuss what had happened—not yet—and then she ended the call with relief.

She only gave a moment's thought as to how she'd handle the face-to-face meeting with her mother next week, when her parents came to Silverton for the Founder's Day Gala.

Cassandra plopped back onto the couch, relieved that the conversation she'd dreaded was over. She didn't bother to turn up the volume on the television. The images cast oddly broken light around the room, but she didn't really care what the people on the TV had to say.

She'd passed many nights just like this, alone in her apartment. But she had never felt quite this alone—not even on her worst days. It was all Kadir's fault, because he'd introduced her to the reality of not being alone. Was it worth it? Was the pain she was suffering right now worth the joy she'd experienced for a few short days?

At the moment she couldn't answer with a hearty yes…but she couldn't answer no, either.

She thought she heard a soft shuffle from the hallway that led to her bedroom. Or was it just misdirected sound from the television? Sharif continued to mumble in the kitchen. Maybe that was what she'd heard. And then she heard the shuffle again.

Just what she needed. Mice! Mrs. Thatcher, who lived alone in the flat next door, had had a rodent problem last year, but Cassandra had never seen any mice in her place. She knew, of course, that didn't mean they weren't there.

Sharif continued to talk to himself, even as Cassandra made her way to the kitchen pantry to grab a broom. While it would be nice to pretend she hadn't heard that soft noise, she'd never get to sleep tonight unless she found out for herself. A broom seemed a proper enough weapon. Her reluctant bodyguard watched her depart from the kitchen with the broom in hand. If he'd been any other man, she might've asked him to handle her mouse problem, but he wasn't any other man—and she wasn't a girl who ran to anyone to fix her problems.

Cassandra stepped into the hallway and reached for the light switch. Before she could flip the switch, a hand flew out of the dark and grasped her wrist tightly. She started to scream, but not much sound escaped before the intruder—not a mouse after all—clapped a hand over her mouth. The broom dropped to the floor as he edged her toward the light of the main room, where the television continued to play.

Sharif stood in the kitchen doorway, eyes hard, mouth grim, gun in hand and trained…on her. Heaven above, she had never trusted that man….

And then she felt the press of cold steel against her temple, and a voice she had heard before said, "Drop it, Al-Asad, or she dies here and now."

Slowly, reluctantly, Sharif allowed his weapon to drop.

"Toss it to the floor," the intruder commanded, and Sharif complied.

Her reluctant bodyguard took one decidedly unthreatening step forward. "Let her go. You and I can..."

He didn't get a chance to say more. The press of steel at Cassandra's temple lessened, she saw the tip of a suppressor as the weapon changed direction and then the man who held her fired. The weapon made a coughing sound, which was louder than she'd expected, but not loud enough to alarm the neighbors. Sharif dropped to the floor, and Cassandra watched as blood bloomed on his trousers, just above the knee.

The man who held her relaxed considerably once Sharif was down, and he allowed her to turn just enough to see his face. She should not be surprised, not after listening to Kadir's suppositions about who might've betrayed him. The first thing she said was, "You shaved."

Hakim, Kadir's timid personal secretary, turned his weapon on her once again.

The phone near his hand rang, and Kadir answered. Sharif was supposed to call every three hours with a report on Cassandra, and he was fifteen minutes late. Sharif was never late.

Kadir said hello, fully expecting another tirade from Sharif on how he should be here, instead of guarding a woman who meant nothing to him or to Kahani.

The voice that responded to Kadir's greeting was not that of Sharif.

"I have them both," Hakim said, his voice distinctly recognizable.

Kadir did not have to ask who both were. There were

only two people in the world he cared about. "Let me speak to them."

"No."

"How do I know you have them?"

Hakim sighed. "Don't be tiresome, Excellency. Apparently Al-Asad did not take your concerns about Ms. Klein seriously. Security was dismal. I entered her apartment through a window. It was very easy to slip the insufficient lock. Once I was in the apartment, she came after me with a *broom.*" He had the nerve to laugh lightly. "Taking Al-Asad was no problem at all, once I had Ms. Klein in my hands."

"I wish to speak with them."

"No, there is no time. If you ask again, I will shoot one of them."

Kadir's heart leapt in his chest. "Have they been harmed?"

"Not yet," Hakim answered. "If you cooperate, they might both very well survive this night."

Anything, Kadir almost shouted into the phone. *Anything at all.* Instead he answered calmly. "What do you want in exchange for their lives?"

"Yours," Hakim answered without emotion.

Hakim had been Kadir's personal secretary for years. Had he always been aligned with Zahid? Had he been blackmailed into assisting Bin-Asfour in his quest? "Why?" Kadir asked calmly. "If Zahid has threatened you or your family, if he's forcing you to do things you don't want to do, I can help. Sharif and I can help you, Hakim, if you'll allow us to do so."

"It's not that simple, Excellency. Bin-Asfour has offered me a lot of money to deliver proof of your death. I won't have to work, not ever again, once this chore is done. I'll have a villa of my own, and workers to serve me and my days of answering to your call, to *anyone's* call, will be over."

Kadir placed a tired hand on his forehead. All this for money. Dozens dead, Sharif and Cassandra threatened, all for wealth. "If you believe Bin-Asfour will part with that kind of money, you're mistaken. He'll kill you without a second thought before he'll part with even a fraction of his fortune."

"I don't believe you," Hakim said gently. "Zahid wants you dead so badly he'll gladly pay anything."

"When did he make you this offer?" After all, there had been many times in the past when Hakim could've put a bullet in his employer's brain. Not without being caught, however.

"A few months ago. Planning an execution that didn't leave me in the hands of your security detail was trickier than I thought it would be."

"So you came up with a plan to kill them all."

"Yes," Hakim said, without so much as a touch of remorse. "Now, quit stalling and let's get to tonight's business. You know where I am. If you're not here in fifteen minutes, the first shot will be fired. If you don't come alone and unarmed, two shots will be fired. One into Al-Asad's brain, the other into Ms. Klein's."

Kadir didn't bother to say another word. He hung up the phone. Before heading for the garage, he yanked up the receiver once again and dialed Cassandra's apartment. Maybe Hakim had been bluffing, and Cassandra and Sharif were fine. He could be ambushed making his way to Cassandra's rescue, when she wasn't in any danger. But Cassandra's phone rang twice, and then Hakim's voice answered with a proper

"Klein residence," which would not alarm an unsuspecting caller.

Kadir didn't answer, and very soon Hakim laughed again. "You now have thirteen minutes, Excellency."

Hakim's last words had painted a frightening picture in his brain, and Kadir could barely think. He did, however, think to grab the six-shooter before he ran from the room.

Sharif wasn't dead, but he'd been badly wounded.

Her next-door neighbor, Mrs. Thatcher, knocked loudly on the door shortly after Cassandra's short scream, and with Hakim's gun at her head, Cassandra explained through the closed door that she'd seen a mouse and been alarmed. The woman was satisfied, and she headed to her flat to call the building manager to make a complaint. She was not going through *that* ordeal again, she vowed.

Cassandra assisted Hakim with Sharif's body. The man with the gun allowed her to bind the wound with a strip of a sheet she'd just laundered, and she worked quickly, since Hakim did not seem to be blessed with patience. That done, they eased the wounded man into a kitchen chair, and Cassandra tried to make sure Sharif was comfortable before Hakim began to duct tape him to the straight back and the legs of the chair.

And then Hakim did the same thing to her, at gunpoint, of course. While he strapped her ankles to the chair, Cassandra pushed her panic down and asked, "You work for Zahid Bin-Asfour, don't you?"

"Don't be nosy, Ms. Klein. No good can come of it."

"Did you murder Prince Reginald?"

His head snapped up. The question took him very much by surprise. "No. Why do you ask?"

"It's suspected that followers of Bin-Asfour murdered the prince. I just wondered..." She shrugged her shoulders, as best she could.

When she was taped to the chair to his satisfaction, Hakim placed his face close to hers. "Why would Bin-Asfour have Prince Reginald killed when the prince had just agreed to align himself with the organization after he took the throne? It would be quite a blow to the Kahani government for Bin-Asfour to be officially recognized and embraced by the throne of Silvershire. Zahid was quite upset when he heard of the prince's death."

"So, do you think someone from the Kahani government murdered the prince?"

The formerly humble secretary shook his head. Of course, she imagined his humility had always been an act. "What difference does it make? You should be worried about your own life, not that of a prince who's already dead."

"I just want to know, that's all. When I get out of here, I might get a promotion if I can shed some light on the murder." In truth, she was merely stalling for time, but if she did get out of here alive, and if she could give new information to those who were investigating the prince's murder...maybe she'd be forgiven for not telling a few secrets along the way.

Hakim left Cassandra and Sharif alone in the kitchen, not that they were in any position to do anything. He was wounded, unarmed and constrained. She was not in much better shape.

"No one from the Kahani government had any part to play in Prince Reginald's death, I swear it," Sharif said in a lowered, less-than-steady voice.

"As if you'd tell me if you knew any differently," Cassandra responded.

Sharif locked his eyes to hers. "There's no reason for me to lie to you about anything. Hakim's going to kill us, you know," he said calmly.

Cassandra's heart leapt. "Maybe not..."

"Even if Kadir comes to save us, which is no doubt the plan, Hakim will still kill us. I just hope Kadir is smart enough to stay away, but I suspect he is not." There was a decided edge to Sharif's voice.

"He'll know it's a trap..." she began.

"And he won't care." Sharif sighed in evident disgust. "Do you wonder why I'm here with you when I should be with Kadir? Do you wonder why I have been guarding you when I should be watching my old friend's back? Do you wonder why I did not attempt to shoot Hakim while he held you?"

"Yes," Cassandra whispered.

Again Sharif looked her squarely in the eye. "Since we're going to die, I might as well tell you. Maybe you should know, since it's come to this. Kadir told me, back in Leonia, that he cared for you the way I once cared for Amala, and that if anything happened to you, he would never forgive me. I care little for his forgiveness, but Amala loved her little brother, and if he loves you then I have no choice but to do as he asks, for her sake as well as his."

"But he..." *He doesn't love me,* Cassandra started to say. The words froze in her mouth. No, Kadir did love her; he just hid that love for his own reasons. "Thank you for telling me," she said.

"You should know, before you die." Sharif sounded like a man who accepted death easily. Maybe he didn't have anything to lose. Maybe he was ready for death. He'd lost his love a long time ago. He shook his head dismally. "I should have taken the shot when I had the chance, but I was afraid Hakim would move and I'd hit you. Kadir would never forgive me if that happened."

Sharif began to work against the bonds at his back, but minutes passed and he didn't seem to be making progress.

Hakim reentered the kitchen, saw Sharif struggling to free himself and raised his gun. He fired one shot, and Sharif went still.

Cassandra gasped, and then she screamed. Hakim turned the weapon on her. His hands were oddly steady, his eyes decidedly cold.

"Be quiet, or you're next. His Excellency is on the way, and it looks as if I no longer need either one of you."

Chapter 15

Kadir parked a short way down the street from Cassandra's apartment building, pulling the black sports car he'd driven to Barton, what seemed like a lifetime ago, to the curb. The security personnel who had been assigned to watch him had tried to follow as he'd sped from the estate, but the sports car was too fast for them and he'd managed to lose them quickly.

He had a few minutes left before Hakim's deadline was over. Now was not the time to panic and rush forward. Now was the time to stop and think. Was Hakim working alone? That was likely, since money was involved and Hakim would probably not want to share, but Kadir could not be sure. He left the car and walked toward Cassandra's building. If he went to her front door he'd be dead within seconds—and so would Cassandra and Sharif, if indeed they still lived.

Kadir stepped into the shadows of an alleyway and dialed Cassandra's number on his cell phone. After two rings Hakim answered, once again using his most professional voice to say, "Klein residence."

"I'm outside the building," Kadir said in a voice that held no emotion. "Give Ms. Klein or Sharif the telephone. When you walk outside and I can see you while I still hear your hostages' voices and know they are well, then you'll get what you want."

Hakim scoffed. "No. You come to me, or there's no deal."

"Then there's no deal." Kadir sincerely hoped Hakim could not hear the panic in his voice. "If I walk in that front door, we're all dead, and I know that well. You're not going to leave witnesses to the assassination if you have an opportunity to avoid it."

"You've just condemned your friends to death," Hakim said solemnly.

"Have I?" Anger crept into Kadir's voice. "Zahid isn't paying you a dime to kill Ms. Klein and Al-Asad. I know you're willing to murder others in order to get to me. Sayyid and Fahd and Haroun and all the other men you knew and worked with, you killed them all to get to me. But if you waste your time murdering Ms. Klein and Al-Asad while I walk away, how does it benefit you? It doesn't. I'm on the north corner, as you exit the building."

"Say hello," Hakim instructed, his mouth far from the receiver.

Cassandra answered. "Don't come up here, Kadir!" she said in a loud voice. "Sharif is..."

The connection ended abruptly—by Hakim's hand, no doubt. Sharif was *what?* Dead? Hurt? A part of the plan, as Cassandra had once suspected?

Kadir dialed the number once again, but the phone rang until the answering machine message came on the line. He headed with a quick step toward the entrance to Cassandra's building. No matter what he'd said in trying to draw Hakim away from his hostages, he would not, could not, leave Cassandra and Sharif in the hands of an armed man who meant them harm.

Before Kadir reached the entrance, Hakim walked out of the building. He was not alone. Cassandra was held before the traitor, and though Kadir could not see the gun, he knew it was there, between Hakim and Cassandra.

It was late at night, and the street was deserted and dark. A lone streetlamp shone down on the three of them, providing the only bit of significant light. Kadir and Hakim each stepped closer to one another, cautiously, slowly. Kadir kept the six-shooter down, slightly behind him and in shadow.

"I'm here," he said tersely. "Let her go."

"No," Hakim responded.

Kadir stuck the six-shooter into the waistband of his pants, there at his spine, and lifted his hands high. "I only want to see the others go free. You can have me. I'm tired of fighting at every turn, I'm tired of watching Zahid win all the time. What do I have to live for, anyway? Zahid took my life from me a long time ago, when he compelled me to sacrifice everything in the name of what he'd done. At this point death will be a relief."

Hakim smiled. "Good."

With a shift of his hand, Hakim allowed Kadir to see the weapon with which he threatened Cassandra.

"Let her go," Kadir said once more.

"No." Hakim's focus was now almost entirely on Kadir, who still had his arms raised. The gun was pointed at him, and Hakim's grip on Cassandra was not as earnest as it had once been. Kadir looked Cassandra in the eye and nodded once, and somehow she knew what he silently asked of her. She yanked once and stumbled away from Hakim. Kadir dropped to the ground as Hakim fired the first shot. He rolled away and drew the six-shooter he'd concealed at his spine.

Hakim was surprised; he'd expected no resistance at this point. From the ground Kadir fired twice. Hakim fired again, but again his bullet went wide.

Kadir fired again and Hakim fell. The gun he'd held went skittering across the sidewalk.

Kadir ran to Cassandra, who floundered as she regained her footing.

"Are you all right?"

She nodded, and he steadied her with one hand.

"Sharif?"

"He's hurt badly. Hakim shot him." Cassandra lifted her head and looked Kadir in the eye. Maybe now she realized why he couldn't afford to love her. By knowing him, by being important to him, she had become Hakim's target. She could've been killed.

The security guards Kadir had managed to lose temporarily pulled their car to the curb and jumped out simultaneously, their trained eyes taking in the situation. At the same time, residents of the apartment building stepped outside to see what was going on.

Kadir turned his attentions to the security guards. "This is the man who planted a bomb on my yacht. I'm quite sure he also hired someone to take a shot at me as I left the Maitland Museum, no doubt to impel me to make the trip to Leonia sooner than I'd planned. A member of the Kahani Ministry of Defense is in Ms.

Klein's apartment, and he's been wounded. I would appreciate it you could call for assistance."

The two men jumped to do all that needed to be done, and Kadir led Cassandra back into the apartment building, weaving past curious neighbors and avoiding all questions. He wanted to take Cassandra's arm, he wanted to steady her. But he didn't. They could not appear to be close, not even now.

Sharif was bound to a sturdy wooden chair in Cassandra's kitchen. He'd been shot twice, once in the thigh, once in the shoulder. The injury to his thigh had been bound, but the shoulder wound was raw and continued to bleed. His head hung forward, limply.

Kadir began to cut the tape that held Sharif to the chair. "The wound in his shoulder doesn't appear to be too bad."

A growl rose from the man seated in the chair. "That's because it's not in *your* shoulder."

Kadir smiled. Sharif was going to be fine. Grouchy, until his shoulder and leg healed, but, still, alive and well.

When Sharif was free, Kadir steadied the wounded man and turned his attention to Cassandra. "I'm sorry you were pulled into this," he said. "This is not your war, and if Zahid's soldiers had any nobility at all..." He tamped down the anger. "But they do not. I'm sorry," he said again.

Sharif lifted his head and looked at Cassandra. Kadir could not help but notice the glance that passed between them, but he could not even begin to decipher it.

"We survived," Sharif said. "For a while there, I was certain we would not."

"I know what you mean," Cassandra said, her voice shaking slightly. "For now, let's worry about getting you to a doctor. Help is on the way."

Sharif grunted. "I hate doctors."

Kadir wished he could feel a moment's ease, knowing the man who'd tried to kill him, a man who had murdered many innocents on board the yacht, was dead. But unfortunately Zahid Bin-Asfour never lacked for soldiers, and he knew another would soon arrive to replace Hakim. Someone else could be paid, blackmailed or seduced into doing all that Zahid desired.

Kadir supported Sharif to the best of his ability, trying to be strong and yet easy with the wounded man. He was afraid to so much as move Sharif to the sofa in the other room, even though he would surely be more comfortable there. It would be wise to leave even the smallest of movements to the medical personnel that were on the way.

Sharif had signed on to this risk long ago. He knew the possible cost of fighting Zahid Bin-Asfour and his followers, and he'd gladly accepted that risk. But Cassandra was innocent in this. She should not be in Zahid's sights, not tonight, not ever.

It was possible that only Hakim knew how Kadir felt about Cassandra. It was possible that Zahid was blessedly ignorant of the fact that Kadir had been foolish enough to think, for even a few days, that he could have a personal life.

Kadir continued to kneel beside Sharif, but he lifted his head and stared at Cassandra. "Perhaps you should wait in the other room," he said briskly.

"What?" She sounded confused, and scared and… surprised.

"Go to your bedroom, lock your door and when people start to ask questions don't tell anyone that you ever knew me as anything more than a representative of my country. You were caught in the middle, you were at the wrong place at the wrong time. That's all."

"But..."

"When I get Sharif to the hospital, I'll make a few calls of my own. As far as anyone is concerned, you barely know me. You didn't realize that I'd survived the explosion until you read it in the newspaper, and it will suit you well if you never see me again."

"Kadir..."

"Go, Ms. Klein."

She stiffened, took a step back and then spun on her heel and walked away. He watched her until she was out of sight. She slammed her bedroom door heartily.

From the bloody seat where Sharif awaited assistance drifted an uncertain, whispered, "I really did think we were going to die...."

Cassandra did exactly as Ms. Dunn asked. She threw herself into preparations for the gala and made sure everyone was aware of the special needs of those dignitaries visiting from other countries. Food, religion, personal eccentricities. There was a detailed file for each and every foreign guest of note.

Her despondency over losing Kadir had been lifted, on that night when she'd been kidnapped and Sharif had been shot. Odd that such terrible events could make her feel better.

Kadir did care about her. He did love her. And even if she never saw him again, knowing that made it all worthwhile. The tears she still shed, the pain she still felt, the deep emptiness she didn't know how to discard...it was all worthwhile. She knew love.

Kadir had only called her once, to tell her that Sharif was well. He'd be out of commission for a while, and was apparently extremely grumpy, but he'd live, and even regain full use of his wounded arm and leg, with therapy. After that—nothing. She'd heard that Kadir would get his meeting with Lord Carrington on Wednesday evening. Would he even bother to remain in Silverton for the gala? He had a new Kahani security detail in place and had settled back into the Redmond Estate, but once his meeting with Lord Carrington was done, there was no reason for Kadir to stay in Silvershire at all.

The news Cassandra had obtained from Hakim, before his death, had answered some of the questions surrounding Prince Reginald's death. Zahid Bin-Asfour had not been involved, and neither had the government of Kahani. There was no longer any fear of potentially embarrassing press to keep Lord Carrington from meeting with Kadir. Who knows? Maybe they'd even form that alliance Kadir wanted so very badly.

It was very difficult to remain angry with a man who so obviously wanted to do good for his country.

Cassandra kept herself busy during the day, but when evening came, her mind wandered to Kadir. Some nights she actually expected him to come to the door and confess his love for her. But of course he didn't come.

On Tuesday night, Cassandra donned her plain blue pajamas and sat down to write her mother a letter.

Dear Mum,

This is a busy week at work, as you know. There's still so much to be done, I'm surprised Ms. Dunn doesn't just chain us to our desks and make us stay until the gala is done.

She hadn't told her mother about the kidnapping, about seeing a man shot, or about learning that Kadir did, indeed, love her. The events of Saturday night had been kept under wraps, and only a handful of people knew what had actually happened. It would be best, however, if she kept her parents away from Mrs. Thatcher this coming weekend….

I do love Kadir. Not that it matters, much. He's going back to Kahani this week. Maybe tomorrow, after his meeting with Lord Carrington, maybe Sunday, after the gala. The sheik and I are too different in too many ways. We could never make it work, and I'm smart enough to understand that.
I love him, and he broke my heart. Even though it still hurts, I'm not sorry. I'll never be sorry. Don't worry about me. I truly am fine.
See you Saturday. I hope Dad got a new tuxedo!
Love,
Cassandra

She sealed up the letter, prepared it to post in the morning, as usual, and walked through her familiar flat, turning off lights and preparing for bed.

When someone knocked on the door, she wasn't surprised. She should've been, given the late hour, but she wasn't. She looked through the peephole, and again, she was not surprised.

Cassandra opened the door. "So, are you here as Excellency or as Kadir?"

He took her in his arms, and that was answer enough. Kadir came into her flat, kicked the door shut behind him and then took the time to lock it.

"Are there guards in the hallway?" she asked. "Spies lurking outside my window?"

"No. No one knows I'm here. I slipped away from my new bodyguards." Kadir laid his lips on her throat and sighed, in what felt and tasted like relief. "It's the only way."

Cassandra put her arms around Kadir and held on. This was secret, she understood that. No one could know…and it wasn't going to last much longer.

"Kadir…"

He placed a finger beneath her chin and tipped her face up so she was looking him in the eye. "No talking," he whispered. "No questions, no tears, no whispered wishes that we know won't ever come true. If you can't agree to that, then I'll leave now."

"You're here just for the sex, then?"

"Yes," he whispered.

She kissed him, knowing that once again he was lying to her, glad for this one last night, trying once again to make memories that would last a lifetime. There was desperation in his kiss, and in hers, but the desperation was quickly replaced by the passion they'd always shared.

Cassandra wanted to take her mouth from Kadir's and tell him that she loved him. But she didn't—and she didn't have to. He already knew.

And she knew, just as well, that he loved her. He would never tell her so, but she knew it to the depths of her soul. Sharif's words, when he'd thought they were going to die, only confirmed what her heart knew without question.

They kissed and took one step and then another toward the bedroom, fingers unbuttoning and unzipping as they went, hands exploring and arousing. Since her clothing consisted of pajamas and panties and nothing else, getting her undressed was easy work for Kadir.

Kadir, on the other hand, was fully dressed. He also carried Lexie's six-shooter, which had been tucked away in a shoulder holster he wore beneath his jacket. As they reached the bed, he removed the six-shooter and laid it on the bedside table. By this point, she was already completely undressed, and several of his buttons and half a zipper had been undone. She lay back on the bed and watched as Kadir finished undressing himself. He had come prepared, and placed a couple of wrapped condoms on the table, there near the six-shooter.

He didn't rush, but neither did he dawdle. And he kept his eyes, his beautiful bedroom eyes that spoke of love even when he denied it, on her the entire time.

When he crawled onto the bed, she wrapped her arms around his bare body and pulled him closer. The sensation of his skin against hers was heavenly, and she closed her eyes and drank him in. He kissed her throat, and then her mouth and then moved back to her throat again. Such soft, talented lips he had. She wallowed in the kiss, and in her body's response.

One hand skimmed her body from breasts to thigh, and then back to breasts again. Fingers raked—gently, barely touching here and there and then rubbing much harder in other places. There was no rush, though her body seemed to spiral toward their joining. It spiraled slowly. Inexorably, but without even a hint of haste. Making love, even for the last time, should never be rushed. It should be savored, and that's what they did. They savored.

Kadir kissed the crook of her elbow, and let his lips

linger there for a moment. The sensation was wonderful, and she smiled as his tongue flickered in and out. He teased her with his fingers, but never too boldly. Each movement was languid, unhurried. Maybe he was making memories, too.

When it seemed she couldn't take any more, Cassandra rolled Kadir onto his back and explored his body as he had explored hers. She kissed his throat and his mouth, raked her hands over the length of his body, searched for those unexpected places where a kiss or a proper stroke made him moan or quiver. Beneath the ear, just beneath his navel, the inside of his thigh.

She raked her fingertips up and down his erection, and then straddled him to lower her head and taste him, very briefly and with a flick of her tongue. It was that flick of the tongue that made him reach for the bedside table and the condoms there.

Kadir made love to her as slowly as he had aroused her. They didn't rush, because they knew when this night was over it would be truly *over.* After he walked out of her apartment—in a few minutes or a few hours—she'd probably never see him again.

So she felt the beginning waves of orgasm with a touch of sadness. Too soon. It was all too soon. She couldn't tell Kadir that she loved him...not if she wanted him to stay a while longer...but as her body cracked and quivered beneath his, she grabbed on to him and cried out his name, and when he came with her, his own completion coming as her body still trembled around his, she said, "I'm not sorry, Kadir. I'll never be sorry."

It was near dawn when Kadir rose from Cassandra's bed, leaving her sleeping deeply and with evident contentment. He dressed without making a sound, but when it came time to return the six-shooter to the holster, he hesitated. The small weapon was not his. It had been borrowed, and it had served its purpose.

Cassandra didn't wake. He could simply walk away. It would be easier than saying goodbye, even if she tried to make the parting easy for him.

He sat on the side of the bed, dressed and ready to go—and yet *not* ready to go. He drew down the covers and placed one hand on Cassandra's bare back. She had a beautiful back, perfectly shaped and feminine and strong. Had he ever told her that he loved the sight of her bare back? As well as the curve of her hips, and her smile, and her feet with the pink toenails, and the grace of her long fingers and…everything. Everything about her was beautiful, and well-loved.

Kadir leaned down and kissed Cassandra's spine. She squirmed, sighed and then smiled in response.

"Goodbye," he whispered.

Still more asleep than awake, she said, "Already? No…don't…it can't be time…."

When she tried to turn over, he pressed his mouth to her shoulder and very gently kept her in place. He couldn't walk out without saying goodbye, but neither did he wish to wallow in the pain.

"You are amazing," he whispered. "There is no woman on the earth quite like you, Cassandra Klein."

She was fully awake now. He felt it, in the tension of her shoulder and the change in her breath.

"Will you be at the gala on Saturday?" she asked. No wonder she didn't turn to face him. Even though she tried to hide it, he heard the tears in her voice. She was not a woman to weep easily, and it hurt him to know he had caused her even a single tear.

"No. After my meeting with Lord Carrington, I'll return to Kahani immediately. After all that's happened, it's for the best."

"Too bad," she said, trying to sound nonchalant and failing badly. "I never got to see you in your traditional Kahani dress."

"Trust me," he said, kissing her shoulder again. "You've missed nothing."

They tried to make light in this last moment together, but could not, and eventually Cassandra turned to him—red eyes and all. She barely lifted up.

"I'll miss you," she said sincerely.

He kissed her quickly, then moved away while he still could. When he reached the door he whispered, lowly so she would not hear, "I'm not sorry, either."

Even though at the moment, he hurt like hell.

Chapter 16

Thursday morning found Sharif Al-Asad a cross, short-tempered patient. All the nurses were afraid of him. He was scheduled to be released the following afternoon, and no one on the staff would be sorry to see him go.

Cassandra arranged the cut flowers she'd brought to cheer up his room, even though he'd already declared that he hated flowers and did not want them in his sight. She'd decided that Sharif was not nearly as irritable as he pretended to be. Maybe he was, but it suited her to believe that he was putting on a show.

When Sharif realized that she wasn't going to toss the flowers or take them with her when she left, he sighed in pure disgust and leaned back against a pile of soft pillows.

"Did you see Kadir last night before he left?" Cassandra asked.

"Yes." Sharif did not elaborate.

Did he think she was going to cry on his wounded shoulder? That wasn't her style, and loving and losing wasn't going to change that. Besides, if she did want to cry on someone's shoulder, it wouldn't be Sharif's. He was seriously lacking in the empathy department. "I hear his meeting with Lord Carrington went very well."

"So I heard," Sharif said suspiciously.

Cassandra quit fiddling with the flowers and smiled down at Sharif, giving him her full attention. He had refused to allow the nurses to shave his face or cut his hair, so he still looked very much like a wild man. The wildness was mostly in his eyes, however, not in his untended hair and scruffy beard. She sat on the side of the bed, startling him with her easy familiarity.

"Since things went so well with Lord Carrington, I expect Kadir will come back to Silvershire, now and then," she said in a lowered voice, so no one passing in the hall would hear her.

Sharif's face hardened. "Don't fool yourself into believing—"

"I'm not fooling myself," she interrupted. "I don't expect Kadir to come riding in on a white horse to sweep me away. I have my life, and he has his, and they don't exactly suit one another well. I've known that all along. There's no fairy-tale ending waiting for us." Still, she had hope—an unexpected, perhaps foolish, girlish hope—that she would see Kadir again. If all she could have was a night here and there…she'd take it. Gladly.

"Why are you here?" Sharif asked, his voice brusque and gruff.

She straightened his covers with a nervous gesture. "To bring you flowers, of course. Besides, I wanted to see you before you go, to make sure you're on the mend and…"

"And what?" he snapped when she faltered.

Cassandra looked Sharif in the eye. "I'll be blunt. No one loves Kadir the way you and I do. I just..." She'd practiced what she wanted to say all last night and this morning, and now the words wouldn't come as she'd planned. Best to be plainspoken.

"Watch his back, please. Keep him safe, if you can." She sighed and once again fiddled nervously with the top edge of the sheet. "I'd like to think that one day soon the two of you will see Zahid dead, or in prison, and I'd like to think when that happens, Kadir will be safe. But that's not entirely true, and deep down I know it. When Zahid Bin-Asfour is gone, someone else will take his place, just as someone else will take Hakim's place. Kadir is so determined to bring change to Kahani, that's all he sees, and I'm afraid he won't take proper care of himself." Again she looked Sharif in the eye. "So I want you to do it."

She thought that Sharif would refuse out of spite, since he didn't like her at all, but instead he said, "I'll resign my post and take over as Kadir's head of security, if he will have me." A crooked smile twisted his lips. "After the debacle at your flat, he might not want me."

"He will."

"I failed."

Cassandra smiled as she stood. "I can't know for sure, but I have a feeling you don't fail very often. After allowing Hakim to sneak up on us once, I don't imagine that sort of thing will happen again."

Sharif's answer was a low growl. She took that as an affirmative, and reached for his unbound hand to shake on the deal, such as it was. Kadir would be in good hands, and nothing else mattered.

"You know," she said as she ended the handshake, "if you had a girlfriend you wouldn't be so irritable all the time."

Her boldness shocked him, and his dark eyes widened.

"You've grieved long enough. Amala wouldn't want you to live your entire life in pain."

"You do not understand the pain of which you speak," he said in a soft voice.

"No, I don't," she admitted. "I can't even begin to comprehend all you've been through. But I do understand love." A week ago she hadn't understood love at all, but now… "Not completely," she added, "but more than I once did."

"Until Zahid is dead, I can't—"

"No," she interrupted. "Until Zahid is dead, you *won't*. There's a very big difference. You're hurting yourself, not him, by carrying all this rage in your heart. I don't think Amala would approve."

Sharif did not agree, of course. Did he ever agree with anyone about anything? Likely not.

But she felt quite sure he would protect Kadir with his very life.

The waves near the villa did not soothe Kadir today, not at all. Instead they reminded him of another bit of ocean, and another seaside home that was not his own.

He had a new security detail in place, a new secretary and a new aide, courtesy of the ministry. Everything appeared to be back to normal—or as normal as was possible, given the circumstances.

His home was filled with strangers…and though they had all been cleared by the ministry, he did not entirely trust them. Would he ever? Betrayal from within was his greatest fear, and that fear had come to pass, thanks to Hakim.

His new secretary, who was achingly young and eager, stepped onto the balcony. "Excellency, you have a guest." The young man glanced over his shoulder, obviously nervous about this particular caller.

Before Kadir could ask who had called, Sharif stepped through the door and onto the balcony, sparing only a quick glance to the vista before him. His shoulder and one arm were bandaged, he used a cane and favored his wounded leg…and he smiled.

"I didn't expect you until tomorrow," Kadir said. "Did the physicians release you early?"

"No, I left on my own." Sharif looked at Kadir and the smile widened. "After receiving a very important phone call." Sharif didn't smile often these days, and never like this.

"What sort of phone call?" Kadir asked.

Sharif did not trust easily, either. He glanced at the new aide, and Kadir sent the young man inside with a nod of his head.

When they were alone, Sharif said, "If you remember, I told you I had a man inside Bin-Asfour's organization."

"Yes."

"I know why he's been trying to have you killed."

Kadir turned to his old friend and waited for more.

"It is his plan to make a move back into Kahani, to establish a stronghold here. He knows no one will fight him as strenuously as you, so he attempted to be rid of you before he made his move."

"You are just as much a danger to him as I am."

Sharif smiled crookedly, and without humor. "I do

not have your influence, Kadir. I'm a soldier who can be taken out at any time, without raising too many eyebrows. You, on the other hand, would be missed. Your death, when it comes, will be newsworthy."

For a moment they watched the ocean. Kadir waited for more—he knew more was coming—and then Sharif said, "I can't remember the sound of her voice."

Kadir turned to his friend. He knew who Sharif spoke of.

"At first I dreamed of Amala often, and in those dreams she spoke to me. In those days I could remember her voice, I could see her face so clearly. Now my memory fails me more often than not, and I haven't dreamed of her for a very long time. I still want Zahid dead, and now that he's in Kahani again, perhaps I can make that happen. But it won't change anything. It won't bring back the sound of her voice." Sharif glanced at Kadir with sharp eyes. "She would like your Ms. Klein. I know that much."

"Yes, she would."

"It's a shame things are as they are," Sharif added simply.

"Yes, it is."

There was a change in the way Sharif held his damaged body, as he changed the subject to that of business. "To continue with the reason for my early release from the hospital and my visit today… We know where Zahid is going to be tonight. There's a rather large drug deal taking place, right here in Kahani, and because it's so large, Zahid will be participating personally." Again, that humorless smile. "Wounded or not, I will be there. No one can keep me away. You?" His eyebrows lifted slightly.

"I wouldn't miss it."

He did know better than to believe their goal of the past fifteen years would be met tonight. Still, simply knowing it was possible lifted his heart.

Sharif turned his gaze to the sea. He sighed, as if he took the same pleasure in the sight that Kadir often had. "When Zahid is dead, do you think we can move on?"

"I don't know."

Sharif sighed again, but without the peacefulness that had marked his appreciation of the view. "Neither do I."

She should've expected everything to go wrong, and all at once.

Cassandra's parents arrived at her flat Saturday morning. Her dad had his favorite tux with him, and he declared it was just fine—even though it fit too snugly and the shirt had blue ruffles down the front and on the cuff. He swore it was not out of style, and never would be. The tuxedo was, in his opinion, a classic.

She managed to intercept Mrs. Thatcher, but wasn't sure she could keep it up all weekend. Maybe she'd tell her mum all about the exciting events of last Saturday in a letter. Someday, *not* someday soon. She certainly didn't want the news to come from a nosy neighbor.

Lexie showed up right after lunch, red-eyed from crying after her ugly breakup with Stanley. There had been a time when Cassandra would've been tempted to remind her sister that she'd been warned about that man more than once. Today she just gave her sister a hug—or two or three—and then rummaged through her closet for a proper gown. The gala would surely cheer Lexie up. Cassandra and her big sister wore the same size, so finding something for Lexie to wear was easy. In the back of the closet hung one royal-blue satin dress Cassandra had ordered from a catalog and never worn. It didn't suit her at all, she'd decided after the fact, but it would be perfect for Lexie. Lexie liked flash in her wardrobe.

Ms. Dunn was in a dither—but that wasn't all that unusual. She called half a dozen times with questions or orders for the coming evening. Cassandra had to be at the palace early to make sure each and every one of the ambassadors was greeted in the proper way. She was not alone in that assignment, but she had to be there.

Lexie helped Cassandra style her hair atop her head, and she did a fine job of it. When that was done, Cassandra reached for the plain black dress she planned to wear.

"You're kidding me, right?" Lexie said as she grimaced at the gown.

"It's fine," Cassandra said. The dress was plain, floor-length, black and simply cut. No one would notice her in the black gown, but that was fine. She was supposed to blend into the background, not stand out in the crowd. The gala was fun, for most, but for Cassandra it would be an evening of work.

"Fine is not sufficient, little sister. I'll wear the black, you wear the pretty blue. I'm in mourning, after all."

Cassandra didn't point out that Stanley was not worth a moment's mourning. To Lexie, he was worthy. Nothing else mattered.

So Cassandra ended up wearing the royal-blue gown, leaving the black for Lexie. She left for the palace, knowing her family would join her later. She'd likely be too busy throughout the evening to spend any time with them, but they had each other. The gala was always a spectacle, and tonight everyone would be vying for a glimpse of the pregnant princess, and there would be a spectacular fireworks display at the end of the ball. It was scheduled for midnight, of course.

Cassandra arrived at the palace early. Along with Ms. Dunn and several other diplomatic aides, she made sure someone would be available to greet each ambassador in their own language, and that the food and drink served to them would be suitable. No fish for this one, no wine for another. No meat at all for that one, and this one had a fondness for fine champagne. One of the ambassadors had gained a reputation for grabbing the tushes of the prettier aides. Timothy Little had been assigned to see to all that ambassador's needs.

Once the guests began to arrive, Cassandra's job was almost done. All she had to do was cross her fingers and hope the evening went well and there were no blunders. If there was a blunder, she'd be available to fix it.

There would be no relaxing, no dancing, no curious peeks at the pregnant princess. Not for Cassandra.

She gave half an ear to the announcements of those dignitaries who arrived. Familiar names drifted in one ear and out the other as she wandered around the room keeping an eye on the ambassadors—and maintaining a distance from Timothy Little's tush-grabbing ambassador. The crowd grew steadily, until the ballroom was teeming with well-dressed guests who danced or flirted or conversed. Cassandra didn't participate in any of these pastimes, but she did listen. People speculated about Prince Reginald's murder and Lord Carrington's marriage. They whispered about royal scandals—some partly true, others entirely false.

Not long into the evening, Cassandra decided she should've worn the black; she drew too much attention in the blue satin. Men stared. They smiled and bowed and even winked. She ignored them all, of course.

She caught sight of her family, once or twice, and sighed at her father in his outdated tuxedo. And then a moment later she grinned widely. He was who he was, and she loved him. Her mum and Lexie both looked fabulous, of course, and Lexie even smiled a time or two. Good. The relationship with Stanley didn't deserve an extended mourning.

Half listening, Cassandra heard the announcement, "His Excellency Sheik Kadir Bin Arif Yusef Al-Nuri…" She spun around and moved to the side so she could see the arriving guests, as the announcement continued. Out of the corner of her eye she saw her mother and Lexie, with Dad right behind, hurrying to join her.

She had never seen Kadir in his traditional dress, not until tonight. He wore a small turban, loose-fitting pants, Kahani boots, a loose shirt and a vest. The colors of the costume were brighter than his usual attire—green and gold, primarily, with a touch of blue a shade darker than her gown. Two men flanked him, and they, too, wore traditional costumes. One was a large, muscled stranger; the other was Sharif. He'd trimmed his beard a little for the occasion, and limped with the assistance of a cane.

Kadir's eyes scanned the room as he stepped into the crowd. It didn't take him long to find her, and when he did he smiled widely.

"Oh, my God," Lexie whispered. "Who is that?"

"That's Ka…" She stopped herself. "Sheik Kadir, the director of…"

"No, no, no," Lexie said, her hand on Cassandra's arm. "The one on the left. The guy with the beard and the stare, and one arm in a sling and a cane."

Cassandra turned to look at her sister, aghast. "Sharif?"

"You *know* him? I take back everything I ever said about your job being boring. You have to introduce me," she whispered as the men drew closer.

"What about Stanley?" Cassandra asked.

Lexie laughed lightly. "Stanley who?"

Something odd happened as Kadir walked toward Cassandra. His stomach flipped over. His heart fluttered.

She was beautiful, even more so than he remembered. All sounds, the faces, movements and greetings of the revelers around him faded to nothing as he moved toward the woman he loved. And he did love her, more than he had imagined was possible.

The blue evening dress Cassandra wore hugged her body and showed off her perfect shape, but that wasn't what made her so beautiful. It wasn't the gown that made his heart flutter. It was the smile. It was the hope in her eyes, as he drew close enough to see them well.

When he reached her, he took her hand and bowed sharply. "Ms. Klein," he said in a low voice.

"Excellency," she responded. "I didn't expect to see you this evening."

He caught and held her eyes. "I didn't expect to be here." He greeted Cassandra's mother, and was introduced to her father and sister. The sister had eyes for Sharif, and she didn't even try to hide the fact. She moved right past Kadir and offered her hand to Sharif.

"And who are you, exactly?"

Sharif's eyes widened slightly. "I am the bodyguard," he responded.

"A wounded bodyguard. That's interesting. I'm Lexie, Cass's sister. Can you dance with that cane, or do you have to stick to your boss's side for the entire evening? I mean, it's not like anything's going to happen *here.*"

Kadir gave Sharif a signal, a simple lifting of two fingers, and then turned to Cassandra's father. "Sir, may I have a moment of your time? Privately, if we may leave the ladies to their own devices."

He walked away with Cassandra's father, leaving three very curious ladies behind.

Cassandra watched the two men leave, her eyes slightly narrowed. What on earth was Kadir up to? Her father, in his too-snug tuxedo, and Kadir, in his traditional costume, walked with purpose toward a corner of the ballroom. Halfway there, Kadir leaned down and began to speak.

In rapid Arabic, Sharif ordered the other bodyguard to follow Kadir but to keep his distance.

Lexie asked Sharif again if he danced.

"No," he answered curtly.

"Oh." Lexie was not one to give up easily. "Well, you do talk, don't you? In English? What happened to your arm and your leg? Were you wounded in the line of duty?"

Sharif looked at Cassandra, casting her a quick, questioning glance. She shook her head very gently. She hadn't told her family anything about that night—and perhaps she never would.

Sharif then gave Lexie a stare that would chill any other woman. "Did you say your name is Lexie?"

"Yes," she said, thinking she had the man's attention.

"Sounds like an automobile."

Lexie laughed, not at all offended. "I suppose it does. It's short for Alexis."

"Ah, Alexis." The name rolled off Sharif's tongue

slowly, and Lexie looked as if she were about to melt into the floor.

Then she sighed. "Honey, you can call me Alexis any time."

It didn't take long for Sharif to quit fighting Lexie and just talk to her. He kept his eyes on Kadir and the oddly dressed man he spoke to with such passion, but he also listened to the woman who was so obviously infatuated with him. Once or twice, he even smiled.

After just a few minutes, Kadir and Cassandra's father headed back toward them. They both looked smug. Satisfied. Manly. Kadir didn't take his eyes off of her, not even for a second. He came directly to her, took her hand and asked for permission to speak to her privately.

A part of her wanted to hope that this was what it looked like…but she didn't dare to hope that much.

Kadir held her hand and led her to a large balcony. There the music and the voices from the ballroom were muted. Another couple shared the balcony with Cassandra and Kadir for a moment, but soon they drifted into the ballroom, arm in arm.

When they were alone, Kadir took Cassandra in his arms and kissed her. Softly, gently, but with more than a touch of real, true hunger. Cassandra sighed and laid her hands on his back. His arms were wrapped so warmly and possessively around her, she reveled in the touch. She had told Sharif that she hoped Kadir would come back to Silverton now and then, but heaven above—could she stand it? Could she bear to hold him and let him go, again and again?

For now she simply enjoyed the kiss. If she was going to learn to take what she could get, she'd have to enjoy the moments when she had Kadir—rather than worrying about how she'd feel after he was gone.

The kiss slowed, and Kadir dropped his arms. "Zahid Bin-Asfour was killed last night," he said as he took his mouth from hers.

Her heart experienced a little jolt. "What happened?"

"Late last night...early this morning...Kahani soldiers interrupted a very large drug deal. Many of Zahid's followers were killed. He almost escaped, but a few of us followed. He did not expect such opposition. After a short chase he was cornered and shot."

She touched Kadir's face. "Who shot him?"

"It doesn't matter."

Him, she thought. Or Sharif...or possibly both of them.

"All that matters is that Zahid is gone. This doesn't mean the danger is over," he said heatedly. "There are others out there who will be eager to take his place. There are others in Kahani who don't want the country to move forward. Some of them will fight. Unless I'm willing to change my name to Joe and hide myself away, there will always be the potential for danger."

She knew him too well. "That will never happen. You're no Joe." He had never fit well into that role.

He smiled down at her. "Cassandra Klein, my life is not entirely without risk, and the lives of those around me are not as safe as I would like them to be. Any woman I love might be a target of those who oppose me. I tried to walk away from you once, deciding that I would not put you in that position of danger, but I was wrong to make that choice for you. You're an intelligent woman, you know the dangers life with me will bring and the choice is yours. I have asked for your father's blessing, Cassandra, and received it. I love you. Will you marry me?"

Before she could answer, an explosion rocked the palace. Kadir's response was immediate and instinctive. He threw her to the ground and held his body over hers. His arms protected her head, and she was completely trapped beneath him. The balcony shook; in the ballroom, people began to scream. She smelled smoke.

In just a few seconds, amidst the panic and screams from the gala guests, it became clear that the explosion had originated elsewhere. Close by, but not directly beneath or beside them.

Kadir rose to his feet and assisted Cassandra, taking her hand and steadying her as she stood. Immediately they turned toward the ballroom. They saw Sharif headed this way, with Lexie and their parents gathered together. He and the other bodyguard were shepherding her family in this direction. Beyond them, there was pandemonium as guests ran for the exits. Kadir moved forward as if to join them.

"Wait!" Cassandra called, tugging on Kadir's hand and forcing him to stop the escape.

He turned and looked at her, his face grim. She saw in his eyes what he expected her to say. The explosion coming when it did might be seen as a sign of sorts. This would be her life from here on out, Kadir's eyes warned her. Uncertainty, the potential for violence at the most unexpected moments.

And yet…

"Yes," she said. "I love you, Kadir. My answer is yes."

Chapter 17

The explosion that had interrupted the Founder's Day Gala had taken place in the medical wing, and it had clearly been intended to kill the ailing king. The comatose ruler had not been injured, but his surgeon, Dr. Zara Smith, had been knocked unconscious in the blast. Dr. Smith had not yet recovered her memory. Investigators were hoping that perhaps she'd seen something before the explosion, and would soon be able to give them a lead.

Those same investigators had quickly determined that the materials used in the medical wing explosion were not of the same type as those used to destroy Kadir's yacht. It was still possible that the same culprit was responsible—that the events of that night had been set into motion before Zahid Bin-Asfour's death—but that was unlikely. Bin-Asfour had tried to kill Kadir more than once, but he had no reason to assassinate an elderly, ailing king who would soon be stepping down from the throne—if he survived.

Those events were days past, and the morning was a quiet one. Cassandra checked her luggage for the third time, trying to make sure that she had everything she needed. It was almost time to leave for the small airport where she had met Kadir a little more than three weeks ago. Lexie had promised to pack and ship the rest of her sister's belongings, but Cassandra didn't want to get to Kahani and find out she needed something that had been left behind.

She'd loved this flat for a long time, and even after the frightening events that had left Sharif wounded, it had felt like home. But now…she wasn't only ready to leave everything she knew behind, she was eager.

Kadir crept up behind her and slipped his arms around her waist. "Stop worrying, love. Anything you leave behind can be replaced."

Cassandra turned in his arms. "I know. I'm just trying to be an organized wife." She wasn't a wife yet, but within two weeks she would be. Her entire family would travel to Kahani for the wedding.

Her heart fluttered as Kadir kissed her. The life he promised her was not the one she'd planned for herself, but it was everything she wanted. Would every day be secure and totally safe? No. Would Kadir protect her? Yes, he would, just as she would protect him.

His fingers tangled in her hair. "Are you ready to go home, Cassandra?"

She grinned. "I'm ready to go home."

Six weeks later
Tuesday night

Dear Mum,
Lexie arrived yesterday, and she's fine. She and Sharif spent most of today touring Kahani, and I believe they have the same activity planned for tomorrow. I offered to show her around myself, but she prefers to allow Sharif to be her tour guide. Finally I think she's found a man worthy of her.

That was an understatement. It was so cute, the way Sharif called Lexie Alexis, the way she hung on to his every word and ignored his occasional glares. Lexie made Sharif laugh. Sharif offered Lexie a sense of peace she had never known. They suited one another well, even though they both still had issues. For once, Cassandra approved of her sister's taste in men.

I hear that things in Silvershire are in an uproar once again. I always wanted to be right in the middle of all the royal scandals, but I'm very happy to be here, instead. Not that we don't have our own scandals, now and then.

I know you always want to know what those scandals are, and what a shame that the Silvershire Inquisitor *doesn't have a correspondent here in Kahani so you can be well-informed. ☺ The man who took leadership of Bin-Asfour's followers after his death is very much against bringing Kahani into the twenty-first century, but he's shut down Bin-Asfour's drug operations, finding them distasteful, and he's in favor of peaceful change. He doesn't agree with Kadir on what those changes should be, but he makes his point by yelling a lot, not shooting people. He doesn't like me at all, but what do you expect of a man who wants to take an entire country back a thousand years? I met his wife last week, and I like her very much. Once the men excused themselves to talk privately, we had a very interesting conversation. She seems to think her husband will come around to Kadir's way of thinking, eventually.*

Wouldn't it be marvelous if two women from very different backgrounds had their say in the changes that were due to come to Kahani? Cassandra knew she would have to take her part in the participation slowly, but still...she was off to a grand start.

From the beginning, Kadir had included her in his day-to-day business as much as possible. They'd made a few short trips out of the country, and they had created their own scandal just by getting married and working together. Talk about photographers! Everywhere they went, around the world, men like Simon York snapped endless photos.

So far, her bare legs had been kept under wraps, thank goodness.

For the most part, she and Kadir had spent the first month of their marriage here, at this villa by the sea. Her fondest moments with him were all by the sea, either here or in Silvershire. She could not hear the waves crash or smell the salty air without thinking of her husband.

Cassandra was living in a foreign country, surrounded by people she was just beginning to know, and yet this was the home she'd searched for all her life.

I saved the best news for last. Kadir and I are going to have a baby. I can't tell you how excited I am, how happy, but I guess you know well enough what a wonderful feeling it is to begin a family. I'm terrified and excited and elated, all at the same time.

Kadir walked up behind her, reached around the chair and laid a hand on her flat belly.

"Feel anything different yet?" she asked, her pen poised above the paper.

"Not yet," her husband answered. "I'll try again in a few minutes." He leaned down and kissed her on the side of her neck, then left her to finish her letter with a wide smile on her face and a new shimmer beneath her skin.

Do you still get those flutters and flips when you look at Daddy? No, don't tell me. I don't really want to know everything that's to come. I only ask because I get those feelings every time I look at Kadir. I know we're newlyweds, but somehow I think they'll stick around for a good long while.

She couldn't imagine ever settling for anything less than what she and Kadir had, now that she knew what real, true love was like. Had she really thought that she could plan how and with whom she'd fall in love? Had she really thought she could dismiss what she felt for Kadir because it wasn't convenient? Trying to stop love was like trying to stop a freight train with a well-placed pea.

Thanks for all the good advice, and the stories about love at first sight. Eight months from now, I'll be an almost-psychic mum like you!
Love,
Cassandra

She prepared the letter to post, and set it on the dresser in the bedroom. Kadir stood by the nearby wide window that looked out over the sea. Cassandra joined him there, wrapping her arm around his waist and leaning in. This was her place in the world, and she would not trade it for anything, or anyone.

Cassandra shared a lot with her mother in her weekly letters, but she hadn't yet mentioned one small fact. Perhaps that fact was insignificant, and not even worth mentioning. Perhaps it was just a coincidence, and to mention it to anyone would be silly. But to her, it wasn't silly at all.

Her husband was the owner of a very fine white horse.

Turn the page for a sneak peek at
ROYAL BETRAYAL
by Nina Bruhns,
the forth heart-stopping book in
CAPTURING THE CROWN.
Available in July 2006.

Dr. Walker Shaw tried to look somber and professional accompanying His Grace, Russell Duke of Carrington, the acting regent of the tiny country of Silvershire, as they strolled through the imposing halls of the Royal Palace toward the medical wing. After all, he was here on official business. Walker's appearance might be a tad disreputable, and his accent slow and lazy as molasses, but his credentials as a consultant with the elite Lazlo Group were sterling enough to regularly be admitted to places mere mortals rarely visited. Places such as this.

It was not appropriate to be wearing the roguish grin of a man with nothin' but romance on his mind.

But he simply couldn't help himself. He'd been fantasizing about coming to the quaint island kingdom of Silvershire for seven years now. To track down and charm the exquisitely sexy and mysterious Lady Sarah—with any luck right into his bed—as he'd done so memorably all those years ago at that medical conference in Italy.

Lord willing, she was still living in her native land. And single.

"I understand your specialty is memory loss," Lord Carrington said, yanking Walker from a particularly vivid memory of Lady Sarah's delicious behind bending over a breakfast tray.

"That's right," he answered, shifting smoothly into his professional persona. "Mainly as it relates to advancing age and dementia."

As a doctor of psychiatry, Walker had spent the better part of his adult life researching the affliction in the elderly. In his flourishing practice, he had treated patients with all kinds of memory loss resulting from everything from psychological trauma to physical accidents to Alzheimer's. Medical research hadn't been his job, it had been his calling.

Well. Until the ugly scandal that had tanked his meteoric career three years earlier put an end to all that.

"I trust it won't matter," Lord Carrington said, "if your patient here is all of thirty-four?"

Walker hardly registered the quick churl of regret at the word *patient*. He certainly didn't bother to correct it. What the hell. He had moved on. And the life he had now was far more relaxed than the one he'd had as an overworked doctor. He was even doing much of the same kind of work—minus the research, of course. With the Lazlo Group he consulted on fascinating cases by day and had lots of free time by night. He'd be a fool to miss his old life.

"Not at all," Walker said, turning his attention to his

newest assignment. "I understand she was injured in the assassination attempt on King Weston."

"The palace bombing, yes."

"A terrible thing. She's a doctor, isn't she?"

Lord Carrington nodded. "Dr. Zara Smith."

"The renowned neurosurgeon?" Walker asked, vaguely surprised. Though they'd never met, he'd read a couple of her papers in the journals. Intelligent woman.

"She's been treating the king's brain tumor. She sustained her head injury saving his life during the blast."

"How did it happen, exactly?"

"Under the plaster, the palace walls are made of stone," Carrington said. "Several dislodged in the explosion, and one of them caught her in the temple. She remembers nothing. Not even her own name."

Walker thought about the relative merits of being able to forget one's past so completely. There had been days over the past three years he'd have gladly traded places with her. But no more. He'd made peace with his demons.

Besides, not for anything would he give up the memory of a certain auburn-haired young lady stretching across an elaborately carved feather bed, bathed in the glow of the magical Italian dawn. If he couldn't remember her, how could he find her?

"Has Dr. Smith regained consciousness?" he asked, getting back to point. The sooner he dealt with this, the sooner he could start looking. And hopefully fill some of those free nights he had….

"She woke the next day. Her physical injuries are nearly healed now. It's just the memory that is lacking." The duke's long-legged stride slowed. "That's why we need your help. We're anxious to have her remember as quickly as possible, so she'll be able to tell us more about the bombing. We're hoping she saw something. Perhaps even the perpetrators." The future king's eyes sought his. The weight of grave concern and heavy responsibility were clearly etched in his young face. "We need to catch these traitors. Silvershire is already in an uproar over the death of Prince Reginald. And now this vile attempt on the life of our king. The stability of my country could very well depend upon the information Dr. Smith might give us."

Walker returned his gaze steadily. "I understand."

Corbett Lazlo, Walker's boss, had given him a bit of background on the situation before sending him in. Crown Prince Reginald had been found murdered at his lavish country estate—poisoned by coLandon spiked with digitalis—and there had been all sorts of speculation in the press about who might have killed Reginald, and why. At the moment the leading contenders were the Union for Democracy, a radical anti-monarchy group that had been steadily gaining political clout over the past decades, and Lord Carrington himself.

In addition to clout, the UD had also been increasingly accepting of violence as a vehicle for political change. On the other hand, before the murder, Russell, Duke of Carrington, unrelated to the present king, had been third in line for the monarchy. Now he'd not only moved up to the second spot, he'd also hastily married the crown prince's finacée and then become acting regent when King Weston collapsed. Two months from now, due to an ancient, quirky law that mandated the ascension of the heir to the throne upon his thirtieth birthday, Carrington would be crowned king of Silvershire.

It all seemed a little too convenient to the country's

rumor-mongers and particularly the local weekly tabloid, the *Silvershire Inquisitor,* popularly dubbed the *Quiz.*

Still, the Lazlo Group's money was on the UD and not the duke, who seemed sincerely reluctant to become king. It was he who'd hired them to investigate both the prince's murder and the attempt on King Weston's life. But it would be nice to have proof of his innocence in the tangled intrigue. Walker could see why Carrington was anxious for Dr. Smith to recover her memory, if he was innocent.

"How long has it been since the bombing?" he asked.

"Just over a week."

Walker pursed his lips consideringly as they passed through a magnificent gilded hall filled with mirrors and tapestries, huge paintings and windows overlooking a formal courtyard garden. A week wasn't all that long. He'd seen cases where it took a year or more for the memories to return. "She's remembered nothing at all?"

"Nothing."

"And your physicians have ruled out any lingering physical injury?"

"Their examinations have been meticulous. Can you help her, Dr. Shaw?"

"I'll certainly try," he said, knowing better than to promise anything. The mind was as unpredictable as the weather in a South Carolina springtime. As they approached the palace medical wing, Walker added, "But there's one thing I need to insist on."

"Anything. Just name it."

"The way I work requires that the subject not be told anything about their former life other than what's strictly necessary. Has anyone talked to Dr. Smith about her background?"

Carrington shook his head. "Just her name, nothing else. Corbett Lazlo already made that recommendation. She hasn't been allowed to watch the news or read the papers, since she has been all over both since the blast. I even managed to dissuade her family from visiting her yet, though it wasn't easy. Her father is the Marquess of Daneby, one of the most influential men and highest-ranking nobles in the country."

"I appreciate his cooperation. The reason for the precaution is to prevent false memories. It can be hard for amnesia victims to distinguish between something they are told and a true memory. We don't want to influence Dr. Smith's recollections in any way."

"No, of course not."

They'd arrived in the medical wing, and Walker glanced around at the compact facility, modern and crisply white. The nurses' station was manned by a rosy-cheeked matron named Emily, whose smile lines indicated she was usually a lot more cheerful than she appeared today. There was a short bank of blinking monitors, cozy furniture and a couple of framed paintings of flowers. No signs of fire or debris.

"You've already made repairs from the explosions?" he asked, surprised Corbett would have allowed that.

"Good God, no," Carrington said, indicating a hallway to their right. "The room where the bomb went off is down at the end. We haven't touched anything, since the investigation is ongoing." He swept a hand in an all-encompassing gesture. "Damage was pretty much confined to King Weston's recovery room and Dr. Smith's connecting office and lab. The stone walks are over three feet thick."

"Is that a fact?" Walker hid a smile, recalling a similar

comment by the nubile Lady Sarah concerning the walls of the Florence palazzo where they were staying. And they'd been grateful for every sound-dampening inch. "I'm surprised anyone even heard the explosion."

They arrived at a closed door and Carrington halted. "This is Dr. Smith's room. Would you like me to go in with you?"

"I'm sure your schedule is more than full, Your Grace, so I won't keep you any longer. Thank you for meeting with me."

With a formal nod and an offer of any further assistance, Carrington strode purposefully back down the hall.

Walker watched him round the corner, then he turned to the door in front of him and took a deep breath. After a quick knock, he entered the room and stood in the doorway, his eyes adjusting to the dimness. The lace curtains were drawn, but the sun was setting on the other side of the palace, throwing the interior of the room into a misty sort of soft focus.

On the tidy bed lay a woman, her long, loose auburn hair spreading across the pillow.

His body gave a jolt of surprise. Or maybe of primal recognition. *There was something about that hair....*

His mind was still working in slow motion when her face turned toward him.

He froze, welded to the spot, his entire being shocked to the core.

Sweet merciful heaven.

It was *her.*

There on the sterile hospital bed lay his delectable Lady Sarah. No longer a young ingenue, but all grown up and sexier than ever, her mouthwateringly curvy body ill-concealed under the thin white sheet, her beautiful face pale and fragile, her sensual eyes wide with apprehension.

She gazed right at him.

Without an ounce of recognition.

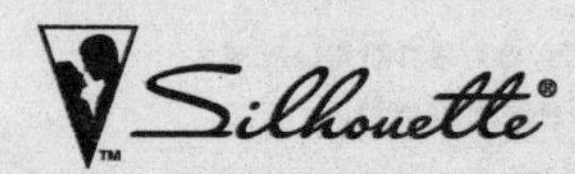

INTIMATE MOMENTS®

COMING NEXT MONTH

#1423 A YOUNGER MAN—Linda Turner
Turning Points
Natalie Bailey is excited to start a new life with her two sons, free of men. Max Sullivan has no interest in settling down. As soon as Natalie enters Max's classroom, he knows he's in trouble of losing control over his desires. Natalie is older, more mature and drop-dead gorgeous, but isn't looking for a fling. Although he tries to resist his attraction, he is fighting a losing battle.

#1424 ROYAL BETRAYAL—Nina Bruhns
Capturing the Crown
Lady Zara Smith barely escapes death when a bomb goes off, leaving her without a memory. The last thing Dr. Walker Shaw wants to do is protect the young vivacious woman he had a brief but magical affair with. But when he realizes Zara is in the center of a deadly royal intrigue, he vows to guard her while fighting the urge to finish what they started years ago.

#1425 DESERT JUSTICE—Valerie Parv
When Simone Hayes returns to the sheikhdom of Nazaar, she overhears a plot to dispose of the ruling Sheikh Markaz Al Nazaari. Simone is ordered to remain under Markaz's protection, while they work together to uncover the conspiracy… and try to resist putting their hearts as well as their lives in jeopardy.

#1426 WISE MOVES—Mary Burton
After witnessing the deaths of six men by her mobster brother, Kristen Rodale promises the police she will testify, until the safe house she is staying at is attacked and she has no choice but to run. FBI agent Dane Cambia wants revenge against the man who killed his sister. His strategy is simple—find Kristen and get close enough to her to capture her outlaw brother. But falling in love isn't part of the plan.

SIMCNM0606